80 Miles

A Novel

Craig Bowler

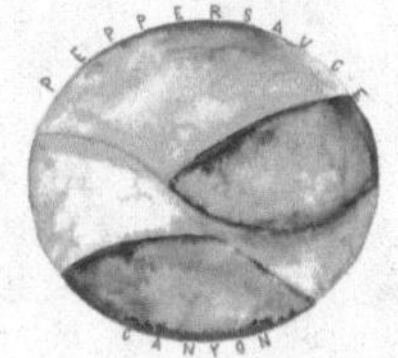

Editing by Richelle Thompson & Renee Montgomery
Cover design and layout by Adele Fogle

Thanks to friends who read multiple drafts of this book and still call me friend.
Special thanks to Josh Cohron who has championed this story from the beginning,
Hunter McWhorter who paid close attention to this story, and mine, and to
Margaret Sims for pulling up a seat at the table. I'm eternally grateful to each of you.

Peppersauce Canyon Publishing.
Printed and bound in Marietta, Georgia. U.S.A.

For Lennon

In memory of Ms. Audrey

CONTENTS

SUMMER 1985

PART ONE - JOHN

The radio station has long faded. The rest of the way to Camp in the Canyon will be silence, static, or this shoebox full of cassettes to see me through.

I wanted to be past this part of the desert by now, but I didn't leave early enough. I didn't see Davis last night so breakfast with him at the Grinder was an absolute. Even though I'm stoked to be leaving, I needed to be with Davis to relieve my guilt from leaving him. Davis needed breakfast so he could remind me he loved me even if I was leaving. At 14 my little brother loves better than anyone ever will. I used the line from *The Wizard of Oz* as we said goodbye, the one Dorothy says to Scarecrow, "I'll miss you most."

A part of me regrets not taking Davis to the party last night. But I knew things would get pretty wild and I didn't want the responsibility of watching out for him. Hanging with Dawn and the crew from fourth period Honor's English class is always a blast. I love being with these kids. We've been together with Mr. Reis since freshman year and the party was the last time we'd be together for a while. Maybe ever. There's no way I was holding anything back.

I'm flying high as I hit the In-N-Out Burger in Riverside. About an hour later I see the sign, "Quartzite 80 miles."

This is the part of the trip I really hate. It's not the heat or the cactus or that the radio won't connect to a station, any station. It's the memory of what first happened in Quartzite almost ten years ago to the day that never goes away. Being out here makes everything so twisted inside, like when you know the best thing you could do is to throw up but you can't. You just have to live with all that makes you sick. That's what this stretch to Quartzite is like.

I know I'll be cool when I get past this. I try to think about anything and everything else as I drive deeper into the desert, but it all keeps coming back. God. I toss tapes around in the shoebox to find something different; there isn't anything. Just static and secrets.

Here it comes. "Welcome to Quartzite."

2.

The sun slips behind the Santa Catalina mountains as I turn off the highway onto the windy dirt road that leads to Camp in the Canyon.

My old truck struggles to climb the last hill to the ridge. The cattle crossing at the peak serves as a victory line, or a starting line. I'm not sure which. From up here you can just make out the creek, my favorite spot in camp. When we were kids, we'd follow the creek as far as light would let us.

As I walk toward the chapel I start to hear singing. I slip in the back and glance around. People are standing, hands raised, a few are sitting with their heads bowed. A couple of kids are kneeling.

The girl leading the song, Beth, sees me and glances to the corner. The guys are over there with some other kids. I'm trying to play it smooth, but am so excited to see those guys. I step over a couple of girls kneeling and then decide it would be more respectful to stay put.

These guys are the coolest guys I know. Genuine, caring, and absolutely hilarious. They certainly know a thing or two about sin, Will especially, but in their own way they're better than me, and when I'm around them they make me better.

Beth leads another song before Pastor Wes Johnson, the new camp pastor from Albuquerque, circles us up to pray. He pushes up the sleeves on his University of New Mexico sweatshirt and grabs the hands of Mrs. Johnson and Beth. He kicks off his flip flops and closes his eyes. Pastor Wes knew my dad when he was at his Sunday best. My dad even mentored him for a while. I study Pastor Wes as he prays: his smiling face tilted toward heaven, his voice calm, with a gentle cadence and tone. He sways, rocking back and forth on his bare feet.

He ends by saying, "God, bless these few days of orientation. Help us to re-orient ourselves to you. And let it begin in me." His "Amen" is the official end of his prayer and the official beginning of summer for me. We all spill out into the night sky.

Me and the guys instantly fall in. "What's up Johnny Rotten?" Will shouts as he comes toward me.

"What's up, Will?" I yell as we throw our arms around each other and then Mark grabs us one at a time giving his best bear hug, "What's up my brothers?"

Pete's right behind him with his giant smile and hugs. "This. Is. So. Awesome!"

<h1 style="text-align:center">3.</h1>

"Let's grab some Cokes from the canteen," Mark says.

I pull out a wadded-up handful of bills. "I'm buying the first and second round!"

We huddle together drinking our Cokes on the dirt road covered in a bunch of high school and college age kids. It's like a party back home. A few kids posing, a couple kids keeping to themselves, everybody else flirting.

Before long, a little crowd forms around Mark and Pete. They're magnetic. Pete is tall and lanky with a freckled face, and a slight hint of his parent's Irish accent. He bounces as he talks. Mark is totally put together, feathered hair, horned rim glasses, OP surfer shirt.

Mark points to the stars, "Look, there's Polaris. See it? It's the end of the Little Dipper, the last star in the handle."

While Pete and Mark continue to impress their growing posse, Will and I retreat and sit on the wall. Will opens his new guitar case already covered in totally awesome stickers, The Clash, MC5, Iron Maiden. He pulls the leather strap over his old denim jacket covered in band patches.

"What's with the Los Lobos patch, Will? I love those guys."

"Did you know they started out playing punk rock?" He lays his guitar in his lap and pulls his hair back into a ponytail. "They don't play punk much anymore. Their new Tex-Mex sound is amazing. They came and played a blazing show at a club back home. They were so tight. So tight! And my ex loved it. Totally put her in the mood!"

"For sure. I saw them with Dawn at a beach festival a few months ago. We had a blast!"

We begin sizing up a couple of girls in the crowd. I nod toward Marcie, who's from nearby San Manuel. She's wearing the Iron Maiden shirt from the concert we went to last summer.

"Think you and Marcie will get back together?" I ask.

"Nah...well maybe. What about you?"

"I'm kinda waiting to see who is out here, you know? Joanna wrote me a few times. She just sent me a letter saying she was going to be at Wagon Wheel again this summer. I never wrote her back."

"No way. I called Sandy the other night...Can't wait for Wednesdays!"

"Oh, God. Wednesdays!"

We hear Mark get excited about some other stars, "The tilt of the earth's axis even effects the tides at the beach." Everyone is taken in. Pete deftly puts his arm around Beth, the song leader, as he points out a small cluster of stars. She smiles, soaking up his attention.

Will shakes his head at them, and we laugh together. Will and I are close enough to those guys where we are, but don't need to be up front with them. I used to be in front all the time. Not anymore. I'm fine right here. Will looks again at Pete and starts playing "One of These Nights" by the Eagles and we sing loud enough for Pete to hear. *"Pete's been searching for the daughter of the devil himself / He's been searching for an angel in white."* Pete looks over his shoulder knowing he's been caught. He turns around and joins in, *"I've been waiting for a woman who's a little of both / I can feel her but she's nowhere in sight."* The three of us laugh at ourselves.

Eventually Pastor Wes, interrupts our little after party. "To your cabins, everyone! May you rest well!"

Mark lingers with Phoebe from Sierra Vista. He's playing it cool as always, but he's totally digging her southwestern vibe. We wait for Mark on the bridge. I quickly dub Phoebe, "Vista" – "She really is quite a view."

Mark shakes his head and laughs at Will and I as we walk back to the picnic table near our cabins, "At least you two will always have each other."

4.

Pete is pouring syrup on his fifth waffle of the morning. "So, I'm standing there before church talking about my soccer game when my ex walks in the back of the sanctuary. I couldn't believe it." The squeal from the microphone tries to interrupt Pete's story. Pastor Wes adjusts some knobs on the sound system. Pete keeps going, "She wanted to confront me about the way I handled the breakup."

I lean over and dip my folded waffle into Pete's syrup, "No way. In church? The perfect place to talk about a break up."

Pastor Wes taps the top of the microphone.

"At least it wasn't at the altar," Will says.

Pastor Wes gets the microphone working. "Sorry about that. Today we are going to do something a little different than the past few days. "I want us to spend the day really getting to know each other." Will groans just loud enough to cause us to smile. Pete and Mark look back at Pastor Wes with expectancy.

"We are going to do some team building activities that will hopefully cause you to rely on each other, work together, maybe even help us be more comfortable in sharing our stories with one another. Andee has divided everyone into teams to help us connect with people we may not know as well."

Will groans a little louder, "This is getting tiresome."

I roll my eyes, "I hate stuff like this. It's like mandatory fun."

I of course end up being on Andee the Camp Director's team. Andee's the worst. She's been out here forever. She looks like she's stuck in the hippie commune she rebelled from in the 70's.

"Circle up, staffers!" she says as she waves her clipboard. "It's time to get to know each other, really get to know each other."

Even though I tried to keep a low-profile last summer, Andee was on me from the jump. And on Will too. She was a constant nag, so condescending and pretentious. We were like her little project. There's nothing worse than being someone's project. She and I had a couple of run-ins and one huge blow up at the end of the summer. "I'm not firing you out of respect for your parents" she kept saying. She knew me and my family from way back and a couple of times she'd tried to talk with me about it. On Sundays, she'd want to pray with me about it. There was no way that was happening.

As we are walking toward the first obstacle of the day, Pete's older brother Danny and I are making small talk when a girl comes out of the last cabin on the hill. She leans on the handrail and waves. I blurt out, "Who is she?" Danny is speechless.

She's stunning. I have no idea how I haven't noticed her before. She must have just gotten to camp. There's no way I would've missed her.

Her brunette hair is pulled back and held in place by her Wayfarers sunglasses. Even from a distance I can see the beauty in her face. And her body. I am completely captivated.

Andee stops and gathers us for an introduction, "Hey everybody, this is Laney all the way from Mississippi. She'll be one of our girl counselors. She's doing a practicum for her social work degree. Make her feel welcome!"

Laney comes down the stairs and all the girls surround her, introducing themselves. Danny and I look at each other. He doesn't say a word to me, but instead he pounces into the small circle gathering around Laney and dramatically slips off his lifeguard visor and bows, "My Lady." She acknowledges him with a smile, reaching out her hand to shake his.

Andee raises her clipboard and says, "First activity of the day is up ahead. Let's go!"

I jump in a couple of times right away to impress this new girl, but quickly realize this is not the way to impress this kind of girl.

It's evident to everyone that this girl is different. Way different. I spend the day watching her, listening to her, totally falling for her.

Before dinner the four of us guys reconnect at the picnic table up by our cabins. When I walk up, Pete is midstream raving about Beth. "Guys, I've been thinking. I may want to get serious with her." Will strums a few chords of "Beth" by KISS, both giving his approval and doing his best Peter Criss impression.

I'm trying to play it smooth, but I'm so anxious to tell them about this new girl. Mark's giving me a look. He knows something's up. I can't help it. I totally interrupt Pete, blurting out, "Guys, have you seen this new college girl from Mississippi?"

Pete looks up and Will stops strumming. Mark says, "I saw her get out of Andee's car last night. She's totally hot."

I'm buzzing. "So you saw her smile? Have you heard her laugh? Have you seen the way she carries herself?"

Will sees right through me and calls me on it. "Hold on, hold on, Johnny Cougar. You know you have no chance, right? She's a college girl. And she's a freaking babe."

"But Will, I'm telling you, this girl has a togetherness that I've never seen. And a wild mix of being totally laid back and yet so elegant."

Pete kindly waves me off, "Elegance? That's a stretch, even for you, John. She is drop dead gorgeous, but I saw her talking to my brother and everybody knows he gets all the babes."

Will is relentless, "Seriously, she's way out of your league. You haven't even made it out of high school and she's not like, community college, or even state school, like the girls around here. She's Ivy League, man. You've got no chance."

Mark smiles. He doesn't say a word. I'm waiting on him to say something. He finally bursts out in a full-blown laugh. "'Ivy League.' You have no chance with 'Ivy League!'"

5.

We pulled an all-nighter, so this morning is rough. Somewhere around 2:30 last night, as we were finishing a game, Will put his guitar down and said, "Let's go caving!"

"Let's do it!" I said immediately.

Mark began to question. He leaned forward on the table, "Caving? In the middle of the night?"

"I've got a flashlight," Pete added.

Will pointed to Mark and me. "Okay, either of you guys have a flashlight?"

I shook my head, "no." Mark didn't have one either.

"I've got one," Will said. "So two flashlights, in the middle of the night, in a desert cave. This will be epic."

It was the stupidest idea we've ever had, and it was totally epic.

Now this morning we are paying for it with total exhaustion. Pastor Wes pulls the microphone from the stand, letting out a squeal that serves as our alarm clock. We all struggle to sit up.

"Thanks for a good week family. We made it to the last day of orientation." A few claps come from around the dining room. I see Danny whisper something to Laney. I try not to stare.

Pastor Wes continues, "We'll have tomorrow off and then campers coming in and out for the rest of the summer. So I'd like to make the most of our day. I want to give you the morning to be alone with God. We'll call it a season of 'silence and solitude.' We'll break our fast later in the chapel."

"This is awesome," I whisper as Mrs. Johnson starts handing out notebooks and pens. I figure we'll meet with God at the picnic table while talking and listening to Van Halen. That's about as close to God as I get these days.

Pastor Wes squashes it. "I'd like you to use this time to find a quiet place to contemplate God's grace. Let's be outside, alone, in the beauty of God's creation. The notebook is for you to journal or write out your prayers to God. Once you get your notebook, your silent fast will begin. Enjoy your time with God."

"I'm heading back to the cabin to grab my guitar and get a couple of cassettes," Will whispers. "You guys want to borrow any?"

"Nah, I'm going to check out the creek," I say.

The other guys stay silent.

I wave at them, "See you guys later."

I end up following the water as it eases down the canyon behind the dining room. It winds and weaves over fallen tree limbs, giant boulders, and a cactus that is out place. The rustling of ivy on the bank of the creek reminds me of Mr. Beaver from *The Lion, the Witch and the Wardrobe*. I keep expecting Mr. Beaver to pop out and excitedly tell me, "Aslan is on the move."

The back gate is padlocked so I climb over the barbed wire fence and wander down further still. The memories of being a kid out here start flooding back. One summer my dad read the entire *Chronicles of Narnia* series to Davis and me. I remember Davis trying to build a dam at the fence line while dad sat on a huge rock and read to us. Davis was like five or six. I was seven or eight, maybe? And I don't know why I do it, but I always look for Davis' bowtie along the creekbank. That same summer we took a family picture on the bridge. My mom dressed Davis and me in matching suits complete with jackets and bowties. She wanted her family back in England to see us dressed in something "posh." They'll never know Davis threw his bowtie into the creek immediately after the picture. My mom freaked. Davis and I still laugh about it.

I love it out here. I always have. It's so peaceful. I lean my head back against the trunk of a big sycamore and open the notebook. Words come fast as I think about the guys and Davis, and Laney. A couple of pages are full when I hear the faint crackle and whine from the camp loudspeaker. I can barely make out Pastor Wes, "Please remain in a posture of silence until we break our fast in the chapel with communion. Worship will begin in an hour."

A few pages later I get up to head back. I jump back across the creek and come up the side of the bank onto the dirt road. As I come up over the hill, I see her, Laney. She's right ahead of me. Something inside me jumps.

I quicken my step to catch up with her. She nods as I nudge my shoulder against hers.

I'm not sure how seriously she's taking this silence thing, so I whisper, "Did you get some good time to journal?" She looks straight ahead, smiles, and nods not saying a word. I shoot up a prayer asking God to forgive me for lusting, for leaving Davis, for homelessness in Los Angeles, and AIDS in Africa, and for every other sin that I've committed in the last hour, or my entire life. And then mercifully she speaks.

"I did," she whispers. "And you?"

"I did, too. I am a wannabe writer, so I used the time to work on a short story."

"Oh, you're a writer, are you?" Still staring at the horizon ahead.

"Uh…We'll I'm no S.E. Hinton or anything…"

She raises her eyebrow an inch and nods. "Oh. S.E. Hinton…*The Outsiders*."

"You know the book?" I ask. "The book is way better than the movie."

"I know the book. Saw the movie too. I love the way Hinton writes."

"Me, too! Have you read anything else by him?"

She smiles raising one eye brow, and for the first time turns her head ever so slightly toward me. "Him? S.E. Hinton is a woman, Ponyboy. Do you know she wrote *The Outsiders* while she was still a teenager? Maybe one day your short story will be like *The Outsiders*. Then I'll be able to say I knew you when."

Total, fail. Oh, my freaking God.

6.

"You write anything during our quiet time, John Hughes?" Will says excitedly. "Check out these lyrics I wrote." He sees Pete and Mark and waves them over to the picnic table. "Listen to this guys."

"Let's hear it, Will," I say in defeat because of my one and only interaction with Laney.

He taps his pencil on the notebook and then swaps his pencil for his pick. He strums a chord and looks up, "I don't have a title yet, but it's about Andee."

"Oh, no." Pete says. "This oughta be good."

Will opens to the first page of the notebook, looks down at the words and then back up at us. "Think punk rock. Get that jam in your heads. You got it?"

He throws his head back and starts singing at the top of his lungs while playing the chords on his guitar, *"She's the pawn, slithering through the lawn, before the dawn, it's Satan's spawn, Satan's spawn!"*

We totally crack up.

Pete tries to high five Will but he's laughing so hard he misses.

"God," I laugh. "She's such a snake! That's so perfect!"

Will says proudly, "That's all I've got so far. What'd you think, Mark?"

"I think we better get to the chapel and pray," Mark says, slapping Will on the back.

We are still laughing a little as we walk up to join the staff all standing outside the chapel. We're a few minutes late and it appears the mood is somber. Andee steps toward us and Will snickers and then loudly hums his new song.

We fall out. Pete bends over and is literally gasping. Mark laughingly slides over to stand in front of him. Andee gives us the look of disgust. I know the look. I couldn't care less.

"So much for silence and solitude," she says in her usual condescending tone. She says a prayer and I try not to listen.

Mrs. Johnson comes out of the chapel and props the doors open. She greets each of us as we walk in. The chapel is set beautifully. Candles light the room and at the front is a huge table covered with a few chalices and all different kinds of breads that give the room the sweetest aroma. It looks like the set from *Jesus Christ Superstar.*

Beth leads us in a few songs. I glance at Laney from time to time hoping she'll smile at me. Each time I look at her my infatuation heightens. She never looks my way. Danny is next to her singing, hands raised, eyes closed. I'm certain he's totally posing, but who am I to judge.

As Beth finishes, Pastor Wes gets up from kneeling at the wooden altar. He moves behind the big table placed perfectly under the cross. "Thanks for taking the silence and solitude time seriously. I hope it was meaningful to you. I want to talk a little about Jesus in the Upper Room on the weekend before the crucifixion."

He starts telling the story, and as he does he moves from behind one chair at the table to the next. I know the story. Everybody does. I go in and out as he talks.

Suddenly Pastor Wes puts his own spin on the story. It's so crazy, he actually sits in one of the chairs and puts himself at the table as if he were one of the disciples eating with Jesus. It's totally insane. He goes, "I'm watching him wash Judas' feet. Judas is so disconnected from what's going on. He's hardly even paying attention. And then Jesus moves to Peter. Peter is crying before Jesus even begins to wash his feet. I'm sitting right next to Peter. I can hardly sit still." He looks up at us from his seat at the table. He's actually getting emotional. "The humility. The grace. The love as the Savior of the world stoops down and takes off my sandals and washes off dirt and grime from the barrenness of our canyon desert."

I can't decide if this is legit, or if all this is a really bad skit from *Saturday Night Live*. But the way he's telling it makes it all so tempting to believe. I look over to see the other guys completely dialed in.

Pastor Wes pushes back from the table, stands, and says, "You too are worthy of a place at this table. He loves you that much. I want to invite you to find yourself in this story."

Beth begins to sing but this time her voice cracks and breaks. I'm surprised. She's always so chipper, the perfect cheerleader. I notice Mark taking off his glasses and wiping his eyes. I've never seen him cry, ever. He's always so together. What's going on?

After the song, Mrs. Johnson goes up to the table and picks up a chalice and tray with bread. She lifts it toward us and says, "You are welcome at this table. You belong here. Come to the table and eat."

Beth, still not fully herself, starts another song. We sit and watch as a few of the staff go up during the singing.

"Let's go," Mark whispers. He and Pete get up and go forward.

Will's smiling as he pats me on the leg. "Ivy League is going up. This is your chance." He gets up fully expecting me to follow. I can't do it. I so want to go, but can't. I'm too afraid the darkness of my heart may somehow splash on all of this.

7.

We jump in Mark's car to head toward Phoenix. "So glad orientation is over and we're finally on the road," Pete says. "I'm stoked to hike Squaw Peak tonight."

"Maybe we can catch a midnight movie at MetroCenter after the hike," Mark adds.

I look up from reading the lyrics to "Shout at the Devil" by Will's new favorite band, Mötley Crüe. "Let's listen to this."

"Oh, it's so rad. You'll love it," Will says. "Let me play it."

Mark is pushing buttons on the cassette player as he drives.

"This reminds me so much of last summer," Pete says. "I know this summer is going to be better, but last summer was the best summer of my life."

"Totally," I say. "I hope we can catch a couple of concerts like last year. That Van Halen/Scorpions concert was so insane."

Will turns from the front seat, "But the Iron Maiden concert at the end of the summer was the best concert I've ever seen. And I've never seen church kids get so crazy."

Pete leans up, "Taking a bunch of church kids to an Iron Maiden concert is dangerous."

"You can't get into too much trouble at the movies," Will says. He slaps Mark on the arm. "Hanging out with a bunch of church kids partying at an Iron Maiden show gets real dangerous."

"Oh, my God," I say. "So glad we were able to crash at Ms. Audrey's after all of that. She saved us. She's excited we are staying with her tonight."

"She's pretty brave to put up with us again," Mark says.

"I think she's the bravest person I know," I respond.

Will turns up the radio. "Listen to this part. Listen. Listen. Listen…right here!" Will stops the cassette and replays the song, now trying to play along with Mick Mars.

I replay my lone interaction with Laney. I know I won't do it, but I've actually thought I might tell Ms. Audrey about Laney.

The next thing I know Pete's waking me up as we pull into Ms. Audrey's. Ms. Audrey waves excitedly from the back gate, "Hey boys, welcome home!" Her weathered wrinkled face gets even more wrinkled as she smiles and hugs us. I can smell her White Shoulders perfume as she kisses me on the cheek. She whispers in my ear, "I'm so glad to see you. I love you more than you know." Something in me rises. I hug her again, even more tightly.

Ms. Audrey points to her little laundry room. We know the routine from last summer. We drop our dirty clothes and head to the kitchen and grab a bunch of

Cokes and chips, then crash in the living room turning on *MTV*.

"Guys, let's skip the Squaw Peak hike and hang out here," Mark says.

I look at Will who is already shaking his head. "No way," he says, "The girls are meeting us at Squaw Peak."

"What girls?" Pete asks.

Will comes alive, "Sandy and Joanna."

Mark leans up, "Wait, the girls from the Wheel? You guys kept in touch with them?"

"John didn't, but I saw Sandy a couple of times," Will says. He sits up straight, "They just so happened to be on break tonight too so I invited them to meet us at Squaw Peak at sunset."

Pete leans over from the couch, "You really think they're going to show, Will?"

He stands, "Of course they're going to show. What girls wouldn't want to be with us?"

We laugh at his confidence and get up to get ready.

Ms. Audrey is waiting by the door with a cooler. "Have a great time tonight. I'll be sleeping when you come in, but let's have breakfast together in the morning."

"Sounds great." She hands me the cooler, "Thanks so much Ms. Audrey." She gently touches each one of us as we walk by.

8.

Cars are parked all over the place as we near the base of Squaw Peak. Mark pulls off the road, and we park in the wide-open desert. We grab the cooler and start down the road. We see a Wagon Wheel van weaving up the trail of strewn cars in the desert. Will waves excitedly and slaps Pete, "There must be a God." The van slows right in front of us.

Sandy, Will's girl from last year, jumps out of the van before it even stops. She throws her arms around Will and gives him the sloppiest kiss.

A few other girls come out of the van. I watch Joanna as she slides across the seat toward the door. She's more beautiful than I remember. She looks like she just walked out of a Van Halen video. Her dirty blonde hair is perfectly teased high on her head. She's wearing a crop top, and a blue bandana tied around her neck. I catch her with a hug as she hops out of the van. Her perfume covers us both. She pushes the hair out of my face as she blushes. Pete and Mark come over and Sandy makes introductions calling us, "The Choir Boys."

"Choir Boys?" Now, that's a stretch," I say to Pete.

"Come on choir boys and girls," Mark says as he leads toward the trailhead. "Let's get to the top so we can watch the moonrise!"

Will and Sandy shoot ahead, arms around each other, whispering all the way up the trail. Joanna and I hang back and soon it's just the two of us and the mountain. Being with Joanna instantly takes me back to last summer. She slips her hand into my hand. I start to slide.

We veer off the trail and find a place that's quiet and shadowed, overlooking the city. Phoenix begins to come alive as the darkness settles in.

Without saying a word, she moves toward me and we start making out. After a few moments, she pushes back and laughs. "Sorry. We'd better start over. I was totally into you last summer. I wrote your name all over my Pee Chee folders and never heard from you."

"I thought about you a lot, I really did. I'm sorry I didn't write you back."

"That's okay. I'm glad we're here together now."

She smiles and grabs my hand as if offering me forgiveness and then we sit and talk into the night. We talk about everything, our camps, our schools, our friends. She asks me about Davis, and then we talk about ourselves.

I point at the stars, "See Polaris there at the bottom of the Little Dipper. Heaven is right behind it." (Mark would be so proud). She leans her head on my shoulder and slips her hand on my leg as we look up into the night sky and further. I lean over and kiss her, slowly grabbing her hand before things get crazy.

"Joanna, you're freezing," I say, pulling my camp sweatshirt from around my waist. "Here, put this on."

"Thank you, John. You're as kind as I remember," she says as she pulls it over her head and then adjusting her bandana.

Pete's laughter, faint at first, becomes louder as he and the rest of the crew walk down the mountain talking about the annual basketball game between the two camps.

We get up and join them.

"'Choir Boys vs. Wagon Wheelers,' my money is on the Choir Boys. They have God on their side," Sandy says. She looks over at us pointing at Joanna. "I know whose side you're on."

The van from the Wheel is at the bottom of the trailhead. The driver honks and waves for the girls.

"Come on over anytime you want to play, Choir Boys," Sandy yells. Will pulls Sandy behind the van to say their own goodbye.

Joanna and I walk to the passenger side. As we hug, she whispers, "We'll be camping out in the canyon on Wednesdays, just like last summer. Come visit, okay?" She kisses me on the cheek and bounces into the van. Sandy follows, all the while blowing kisses at Will.

Pete with his signature innocence asks, "Hey Will, what happened to you and Sandy? We lost track of you. You too John."

Will's grinning, "Nothing happened," he says. "She asked me to kiss her, I said no. You know the drill." He pauses and gets still. "Guys, I can really see myself with a girl like Sandy someday."

"Why is that?" Mark asks.

"She's so different than Marcie. Sandy is confident, a little mysterious, and really sexy."

I get still myself, "Joanna has a couple of those qualities. Laney has all of those."

Will punches me in the arm, "You'll never know."

9.

The morning brings the best smell of the summer. Ms. Audrey's busy in the kitchen when I come downstairs.

"How are you, John?" she wipes her hands on the apron covering her hospital uniform. "You look good," she says as she brushes my wet hair out of my face.

"I am good, Ms. Audrey. Thanks so much for everything. I really appreciate it. The guys do too."

She motions for me to grab the French toast and eggs. The guys come down and join us at the table. We begin to devour everything in sight.

While we eat Ms. Audrey tells stories about her trips to Kenya, her impending retirement, and her hopes to volunteer more at her little church.

In the middle of a story about her plans to hike the Grand Canyon with her sister, she slows down and grabs my arm. She leans in toward me and says, "You know if you ever need to talk, or need a break, or need a Coke..." she stops in mid breath. She draws closer again and this time places both hands on my arm, "John, you are exactly what God had in mind when He created you."

I pull away, not really comprehending what she said. I look across at Mark as a smile takes over his face. Ms. Audrey doesn't budge until finally she motions toward the French toast. "Pass the toast, please, Will."

We sit still, but not silent. If what she says is true, it's true for each of us. But how could it be? No one speaks. No one even moves. Will is staring a hole through his plate. I catch Pete look toward Ms. Audrey. They lock eyes. They are beaming at each other.

Ms. Audrey leans in and places her arms on the table, locking her fingers together just below her chin and says, "When you boys think about heaven, what do you think about?" Tears fill her eyes. "My husband is there you know. I think about heaven a lot."

God, I remember the night he died. It was my first introduction to grief. Real grief.

She looks at me and smiles, then looks back at Pete. "Pete, when you think about heaven what do you think about?"

"Wow. That's big." He pauses. "I don't know...I think about innocence lost that I'll find again. Innocence that was taken. Innocence given back to people that I've taken it from."

"Yes. That's powerful, Pete," Ms. Audrey says. "What else?"

"I don't know. I think about soccer and the beach and music and beauty, I guess." He slides back in his chair and then he says, "I think about my grandma. Maybe she and your husband are having French toast together up there today."

Ms. Audrey wipes a few tears from her eyes and smiles. We sit in the silence; somehow this all feels really holy. Ms. Audrey's beeper goes off, startling all of us into slight laugher. She excuses herself and points to our laundry folded in stacks on the couch.

"We'd better get going," Will says. "Before she asks us any more questions."

We clean the table and gather up our laundry and take a few things to the car. I wash some of the dishes as she hangs up the phone.

She grabs a pencil and points to the calendar on the door, "John, when will you guys be back home?"

"Our next long break is in two weeks."

She writes, "Boys Home" across the boxes and follows us out the back gate. She hugs everybody and me last. "I love you," she says loud enough for the guys to hear, "You are exactly what God had in mind when He created you."

"Thank you, Ms. Audrey. Love you too." I smile as we all get in the car.

Pete and I stretch out in the back seat. We are quiet for a while as we drive out of Phoenix and then Pete looks over at me and says, "I don't know what it was like to have a meal with Jesus. Like to actually sit there and have a meal with Jesus. I don't know what that felt like, or sounded like, or even tasted like, but for some reason I think it might have felt like that breakfast, back there."

"Wait, with Ms. Audrey?"

"Yeah. I think. Pretty much so."

Will turns around from the passenger seat and leans his arm over and says, "So, you think the disciples and all those guys felt like that when they ate with Jesus?"

Pete nods at Will and then asks me, "I don't know. What did it feel like for you when you were sitting there?"

"I don't know. She totally floored me."

"So, what did it feel like?"

"Seriously?"

"Yes. Seriously!"

"I don't know…it made me feel…I don't know, special…God that sounds so stupid."

Mark, totally engaged, speaks to me through the rearview mirror, "There's nothing stupid about it, John. I have no idea what it really felt like to be with Jesus, but wouldn't it feel special?"

I look at Pete. He's smiling. Mark's smiling too. "I'm a little lost. I mean, He's Jesus and everything so it wouldn't feel like hanging with Ms. Audrey would it? That seems way too ordinary."

Mark says, "It felt real. It felt honest. It felt…special."

Will is playing a few chords, nodding with the music, "I hear you guys. I can see Jesus asking questions like that. I'd be afraid that I'd get them wrong and He'd kick me out of the band."

"Would Ms. Audrey kick you out, Will?" Mark asks.

He sighs a little and then smiles, "I mean if she knew her boy over here is in love with Ivy League, she might." We all laugh, mostly in agreement.

I love this kind of stuff with these guys, these kinds of conversation. This sort of wrestle is so good. So good.

Leaning in I say, "Guys honestly, if Ms. Audrey knew all the b.s. that I've done in the last few years, she'd definitely kick us out. There's no way she'd say all that stuff she said. She wouldn't. She couldn't."

Pete slaps me on my arm, "Nah, I don't think so, John. I think if she knew the truth about all of that b.s., she'd actually love you more, if that's even possible."

I blurt out, "Come on dude. No way."

"Seriously," Pete says. "I don't know if there is anything you could do that would cause her to kick you to the curb. You could walk away from her, but I don't think she's going anywhere."

Will laughs, "I hope not. Then where would we get our laundry done?"

Mark is waving his hand and nodding. He's smiling bigger as he talks through the mirror. "I think you're right, Pete. She's not going anywhere. If anything, she's coming toward us."

It's quiet for a few moments. I notice the sagebrush blowing in front of the saguaro cactus as it stands at attention. Ms. Audrey's words are circling in my head.

Will punches Mark's arm, "Okay, but can we talk about Johnny Cash being 'exactly what God had in mind when He created him.' That's ridiculous."

"I totally agree," I say, "That's totally insane."

Mark starts nodding again. He's almost laughing as he talks. "I don't know guys. Think about it. Think about it," He starts tapping his hand on the steering wheel, "No, for real. What if we are exactly what God had in mind when He created us?"

Pete's with him, "Totally. What if Ms. Audrey is right? What if He loves us exactly as we are, not for who we will be one day, when we get less sinful and more spiritual. I don't know. I like it. 'I'm exactly what God had in mind when He created me.' That's awesome."

The car takes on a different kind of quiet. It seems Mark and Pete have this totally figured out. Will turns up the radio and leans his head back. He taps his finger along with the music. My head is spinning. It's all over me. If there is anyone in the world who is actually like Jesus, it's for sure Ms. Audrey. But there's no way I could be exactly what God had in mind? After everything that's happened? After everything I've done? After everything that's been done? There's no possible way that this is what He had in mind. The rest of the drive is pretty staid, save the Vince Neil's screaming vocal on "Too Fast For Love."

10.

Pastor Wes and Mrs. Johnson are up near the parking lot greeting the staff as we come back. Pastor Wes ducks his head in the window, "Welcome home boys. We are so glad to see you. We are praying for you and the rest of our summer together." He pulls his head back out and taps me on the arm. "See you in the staff lounge at noon."

As we park the car, Pete starts talking about the Johnsons. "I think he's pretty cool. I was psyched the other day when he told the communion story. That was cool. I never thought about actually being in the story like that."

"Me either," Mark says. "I always assumed it was an old Bible story, but when he did that the other day, it changed the whole thing. It hit me, for sure."

"It did make it real for once," I add. "But is it okay to do that? Like, is it cool to change the story like that?"

"I think so." Pete says. "I think it's actually a pretty cool way to view the whole story. View it as if you were in it."

Mark takes it a step further. "That guy is not viewing as if he *were* in it. He's talking about living it as if he *is* in it."

<h1 style="text-align:center">11.</h1>

We hustle into the staff meeting and because we're late we sit right inside the door. I immediately look for Laney. She's directly across the room from me. She's huddled up with Danny, Andee, and Crafty, who works in the Craft House (I think her name is Eileen, but I'm not sure). Laney looks so at ease. So relaxed. She looks across the room right at me, but doesn't see me. She looks right past me.

Pastor Wes starts to talk about the kids that will arrive later this afternoon. "I'm excited about each group that will come in this summer. All four groups are from different places in the southwest. They'll look different, dress different, talk different, but I want you to know the heart is the same. No matter the face, the heart is the same. This first group of campers are coming from South Mountain. It's largely a Hispanic population. I can't wait to meet these kids and get to know their stories."

I know South Mountain. We played soccer there a few times. It was pretty rough back then.

Pastor Wes keeps going. "During my talks in this camp I'm going to ask a series of questions that God asked to some of his favorite people. I want to ask you one of those questions now and give you an hour or so to think about it. I'd like you to really think about it and then meet me in the chapel, prepared to respond." He looks at Mrs. Johnson, who is smiling big, with a really old Bible open on her lap. He nods at her and she begins to read.

"Jesus said, '*Come to me all who are weary and heavy laden and I will give you rest. Take my yoke upon you and learn from me and you'll find rest. Rest for your souls.*'"

As she's reading, Bernice, the camp secretary, comes in quickly and whispers something to Pastor Wes. Mrs. Johnson finishes her reading and smiles as if she's discovered something wonderful. She looks up, watching Bernice and Pastor Wes. Pastor Wes nods, and looks directly at me. My heart sinks.

"John, your brother is on the phone in the office. It sounds urgent." I don't know what he said after that. My mind floods with what could have happened. My body responds instinctively and I sprint the 50 yards across camp to the office. I know it's my mom. It's always my mom. *God, now what has she done?* I grab the phone as it sits alone on the desk.

"Hey, Davis," I say out of breath, but trying to be cool. "What's up man, you okay?"

"Hey, Big. I'm sorry to call. I don't know what to do. It's mom."

"No, no. It's cool, lil' bro. You know you can call anytime. Tell me what's up." I try to catch my breath.

"I don't know. Mom's straight trippin'. She and Mr. Terry got into it again, big time. They were down at the Grinder having pie and mom went crazy and started shouting at him and I guess started hitting him. The cops came and everything, dude."

"So, is she home, or…?"

He interrupts. "No, she didn't come home last night. I waited for a few and then went up to dad's. I skated back down to mom's a bit ago, but she's not here. Looks like she hasn't been home. I'm freakin' a bit, Big."

"Oh, man, bro. She's probably up at Mr. Terry's I bet…this is so stupid. God, when is she going to get it together?"

"I don't know. I did hear she clocked ol' boy pretty good though."

"No way? Did she go all 'Thunder Lips' on him like last time?"

He tries to laugh. "My boy at the Grinder said mom was going crazy. He said she threw Mr. Terry's cowboy hat straight at the salad bar. My boy said it would have been hilarious if it was someone else's mom."

"For real, man…it's never someone else's mom, is it lil' bro?"

There's a long silence and then he says in the most defeated voice, "Nope, dude. It's always our mom. What do you want me to do? Should I call the cops and see if they arrested her?" He starts choking up. "Should I call the hospital?"

"Come on man. I'm sure it's not that crazy. Let's not go there again. Davis, honestly, I don't know. And I don't really care about her. I'm more worried about you. I'm way over here and left you with all this."

"Nah, nah. I got this. You do your thing. You finally got out of here for a while. Just tell me what to do? I can handle it."

The door to the office swings open. Andee and Bernice have been talking outside and are now barging in. I feel invaded as Andee gawks at me with her disdainful smile, but it wouldn't have mattered how she looked at me. I turn away to the corner to cover my nakedness.

I try and talk with some form of privacy, but know I'm totally exposed. With almost a whisper but with a tone of assurance I say, "Listen, I can head out now and be there by midnight."

He interrupts me again. "Come on, Big. You don't need to do that. I got it… should I tell dad?"

"Nah. Let's leave dad out of it. That dude doesn't need this b.s. either. Leave it alone for now. Call me back when you hear something. If I don't hear from you I'll call you tonight a few minutes before our curfew. Is that cool?"

"Yeah, man. That's cool…you have a curfew, bro?" He laughs, "You got a back window to sneak out like at dad's?"

"This guy! Come on now, you know this is about Jesus and stuff!"

He's cracking up. "Jesus is all about the curfew."

I start stalling. I don't want to hang up. "Yeah, He is." We both laugh. "You good, lil' bro? You good?"

"You know I'm fine. You good, Big?"

"I mean, I'd be better if mom knocked out old boy. We may need to give her some tips. Like the way you clocked dude on the Bucs last season."

"Oh, that dude had it coming. That kid is a punk. I saw him at the arcade the other day. Lil' punk ass."

"For sure, man. You let me know, okay. You call me anytime." I try to hold it together but I am struggling. "Hey, you know I love you little bro. Man, I love you."

"I love you too, Big." I can hear him choking up as he hangs up. Tears begin to fill my heart, and then my eyes. I won't let Andee see them. Any of them.

<h1 style="text-align:center">12.</h1>

"You should probably go home and try and take care of that, whatever that is. We really don't need you here," Andee hisses.

"Thanks for caring so deeply, Andee. Your concern for my family is such a blessing."

"I'll let that go. I know you are speaking from a place of hurt, as usual. I think you and your family – and our camp family – would be better if you were back in California."

I put the phone on the desk, stand up, and walk toward the door.

"John, don't you walk out. If you walk out on me…" I don't care to hear the rest of what she has to say. I blow past her, swing open the door and walk out. Pastor Wes is up on the dirt road talking to Mrs. Johnson and Beth. I ignore him as he waves at me. Will's down on the basketball court shooting baskets and when he sees me he grabs his guitar leaning up against the fence and jogs up, getting in step in seconds. We walk away up toward the cabins together.

I start grabbing stuff and throwing it on my bed. Will hands me my box of cassettes.

"So, how long are you leaving for?"

"I don't know. Maybe a couple of days, maybe for good? I don't even know."

"For good? Come on John Fogerty, you're making some progress with Ivy League. I mean, not much progress, but there's a chance, right?" He laughs at himself.

"Stuff with my mom is out control and my little brother is carrying it all. I should go home and see what's up."

"No, you don't need to go home. Your mom is always out of control. You need to let all of that craziness be crazy. You can go home on the next break if you need to. I'll even go with you if you want. We all will."

Pastor Wes knocks on the door as he walks in. "Boys, everything okay?"

Will shoots back, "John's family is going nuts again and now he's going nuts. Maybe you can talk some sense into him." He slaps me on the back and walks out.

Pastor Wes puts his hands in his pockets and leans against the doorframe. "What's going on, John? Tell me about the conversation with your brother."

"It's fine, Pastor Wes. My mom is having a hard time. My brother said she didn't come home last night. I can't leave him with all of this. I should get home and help take care of it."

"Oh, John. I'm so sorry. You go home if you think that's the right thing to do. I think it might be best for you to stay."

I look at him for the first time. "Andee says it might be best for me to go."

"I disagree. You belong here as much as anyone. Tell me about your mom.

What's happening with her?"

"She freaked out again and didn't come home last night. My brother doesn't really know what's going on. He's going to call me when he hears something."

"Then why are you going home now?"

"Because he needs me and he's my responsibility."

"He does need you, but he can lean on your dad and other friends there. You don't need to fix this, John. You can't, really."

I want to argue with him but I don't want to argue with him.

"So, he's going to call back?" Pastor Wes asks. "Why don't you stay here and plan on being here until he calls? Take one day at a time, John. Jesus said that a few times, you know? He's usually right."

"Usually."

"Listen, I want to invite you to consider your story. I know much of your world has been wrapped up in the story of your parents. I want you to stay so you can begin to live into your own story. So, take some time. The staff will meet up at the chapel in half an hour. We are going to have a special time of worship before the campers arrive, and I'd like you to be there. At least come and worship before you make any other decisions. You okay with that?"

13.

The chalkboard sign reads, "In attitude of worship, please remove your shoes. You are standing on holy ground."

I'm purposefully late after going down and shooting baskets. As I grab the handle on the door, the singing stops. I hear Andee begin to pray and let go. There's no way I'm listening to another word from her.

I walk away from the chapel and toward the parking lot. So much of me wants to leave. I'm pretty good at leaving. I suck at staying. Seems like I've lived most of my life in the land in between.

I lean over the bed of the truck and fumble with my keys. I realize my cassettes are back in the cabin. I'll never make it through the desert static without some distraction.

A faint horn blows from the ridge above. I squint to see what's coming. The horn sounds again and this time it's joined by cheers and screams of excitement. Soon I can see one, then two, three, four, five yellow school buses coming over the ridge and down toward camp. The sounds of expectation from these kids washes over me. I slip the keys back into my pocket.

14.

"Man, Pete. I'm pretty pumped about being with these kids, and pretty nervous. I hope I don't mess these kids up," I say as Pete and I walk toward the buses.

"What are you talking about? You're great with kids."

"Get out of here. I have no idea. I can't even help my own brother, and now I'm supposed to take care of these kids."

He slows and looks at me, "You okay, John?"

"It's good. Just stuff back home."

"I know it, dude. I do." Pete says, "I don't know really know all about your stuff, but it sure sounds a lot like mine."

He catches me off guard. "What do you mean? You still got stuff going on back home?"

"Yeah, man. It's all over the place."

Kids start jumping off the bus ahead of us. I'm not sure now is the time, but I have to ask, "So, I got your letter last month about becoming a Christian and stuff, but you haven't talked about it much."

He stops walking and laughs a little, turning toward me. "Yep, I got all kinds of stuff going on back home. And following Jesus has actually made things messier for me. Better, but messier."

"That sounds backward."

Will's shout interrupts us, "Pete, John. Get over here!"

The scene ahead of us is pretty chaotic. Will's got a kid hanging on his back. Mark is hugging kids like he's Santa. A suitcase comes flying out of the bus window. Will yells again, "John! Pete!"

We jog toward the buses, both of us energized by the frenzy but still very much in our conversation.

Pete looks over and points ahead. "I guess it's a lot like this." He's practically yelling, and now he's beaming. "Totally excited. Bringing all my baggage to Jesus. Leaving it there. Then it's like walking into a new place, a new space, and seeing what might happen. Just being free. I have absolutely no idea what's going to happen, but I'm so stoked to find out."

15.

We dodge flying beach balls while corralling kids into the chapel.

The thumping music slowly fades, but the enthusiasm only swells, "Counselor Pete and Counselor Beth, come on down!" Everyone cheers like these two are their favorite celebrities. The music cranks up again and Pete and Beth do the pogo dance, jumping up and down all the way down the aisle. All of us jumping with them. Five more seconds and a mosh pit will break out!

Pete and Beth meet their campers and grabbing hands make a grand exit full of cheers and beach balls and bubbles popping from a giant bubble machine.

"Counselor Laney, Counselor John, come on down." I bounce up the aisle. Laney's already on the stage clapping and high fiving kids, so I do the same.

I'm buzzing. Because Laney and I are called up together, that means our kids are about the same age, and we'll probably overlap during our day. I'll get to see her a bunch. This is awesome!

I meet my guys, each dressed alike: new crisp white T-shirt and tan Dickies pants. Slicked black hair. A couple guys are wearing hair nets. One guy has on rosary beads. These guys are from South Mountain but they look like kids back in Boyle Heights in east L.A. or the opening band at a Los Lobos concert.

"Let's get out of here, guys. We've got a lot to do today!"

One of the boys asks expectantly, "When do we eat?"

"Later this afternoon we'll get to go to the World's Largest Ice Cream Sundae."

"No way, homie! For real?"

"For real. But first we've got to get to the cabin and get our swim shorts on for a quick dip in the pool."

"Vamanos!" he yells.

We hit the pool, the basketball court, and then back to the field for the ice cream sundae. As we walk up one of my guys yells, "This is heaven!"

Brian from the kitchen hands us each a bowl and plate, "Have as much as you want, fellas. This is all for you!"

My guys are grabbing burgers and ice cream as fast as they can. All I can think about is the meal from *Babette's Feast*.

One kid keeps saying, "This is the coolest day of my life homies. I can't believe I get to have as much as I want! I never get to have seconds. This is the coolest day of my life!"

I'm scooping up my own sundae next to a kid who has more whip cream than ice cream in his bowl, when Pastor Wes walks up. He motions for me to step back with him. "Hey John, your mom called a few minutes ago. She left a message with Bernice. All is well. She's fine. She said your brother got a little worked up and made things out to be worse than they actually were."

"What about Davis?"

"Your mom says everything is fine."

"She always says everything is 'fine.' She's never been fine."

"Listen, we need you here." He nods toward my campers, "These guys need you here. As much as you can, I want you to leave all of that stuff back in L.A. and live into the stories here."

"I hear you. Is it cool if I give Davis a call later?"

"Sure, John. Anytime," he says as I turn away.

16.

The only thing I remember from last summer is kids like it when someone calls them by their name – better yet, the boys love it when a girl calls them by name. I decide that each time I learn a name, I'm going to immediately find a girl and make an introduction.

I've been doing it all day, and these guys are having more fun with this than the ice cream and burgers. They're pulling on me whenever we cross the path of a girl's cabin. "Introduce me, homie. That girl, that one right there!"

Juan is cracking jokes to his homies as Beth and her girls walk toward us. He grabs my arm. "Talk to her, ese! Her. That girl!"

I stop one of the girls. "Hey, can I talk to you for one second?"

All of her friends circle around. They're giggling their 13-year-old giggle. Beth's even laughing but keeping close watch over these girls like a mother hen.

I lean a little closer to this girl who's wearing way too much make up for any girl, let alone a 13-year-old. "What's your name, sunshine?"

"Vanessa." She giggles again. Her giggle makes me giggle.

"Vanessa, you see this kid right behind me?" She shyly nods. "He's the coolest kid in all of camp." She peers around me. "His name is Juan, but we all call him 'Booger.'"

All the girls squeal. Juan jumps on my back and yells, "You're a jerk, John!" Everybody laughs as the girls head up the dirt road and we romp down onto the basketball court and meet up with Pete and his crew. My guys start shooting trick shots and trying to figure out how to dunk the basketball. Booger crawls up Jimmy and sits on his shoulders. We laugh at them and then Pete runs over and crawls up on my shoulders. We try to block their shots and then I run us into Booger and Jimmy. We grab each other but all four of us fall onto the court, now laughing harder than ever while writhing in pain.

"Camp is awesome, homie!" Booger yells.

17.

At dinner, my guys are almost quiet. It's not because they don't have anything to say; it's because they're stuffing their mouths as fast as they can. I figure this may be my only chance to talk, without the group going crazy, "Homies, let me lay down a couple of rules for our cabin."

Lonny, a heavy-set kid who's tight with Booger, raises his hand.

I pull his hand down, "What are you doing? You don't have to raise your hand here."

He tugs at the collar of his white T-shirt, "Oh, okay, um, Counselor John, is there a rule on how many burritos we can have?"

I glance at Lonny, and then at all the guys, "No, there's not a rule. Yes, you can have more. Chill, they'll bring some more in a minute."

Booger raises his hand as he sips some milk out of the small carton. He looks straight at me and puts the carton down and lets out the loudest burp I've heard in a long time. The whole table cracks up. I try not to laugh, but I can't keep it in. I look over my shoulder and see Andee stand up to see what's happening. They all see me looking at her. Booger nods, "Can that ol' lady get us some more milk too?"

I lean my head down toward the center of the table, "God, that ol' lady is my boss. She doesn't bring food. She brings the law. But yes, you can have more milk, you can have as much as you want."

Booger smacks Lonny, "Then let's eat like we are homeless!"

Andee begins circling the room, coiling up to strike.

I sit up and try and regather this crew. "So, back to the rules," I say, "First, you can have as many burritos as you want, but you can't fart in the cabin." They didn't laugh. At all. Noted. "Second rule, you can't go into anyone else's cabin. Only our cabin. You got it? This is a big one. If you get caught in a girl's cabin, you'll get sent home."

They all amp up. One liners begin coming from everywhere.

"What do you consider 'in' a girl's cabin?"

"My girl won't sleep if I don't give her a goodnight kiss and tuck her in."

"Then who's going to do my laundry?"

Booger waves all the other guys down, "But the girls can come into our cabin, right? We can make out on my bed. That's cool, right?"

I try not to laugh but these guys are firing stuff so fast I can hardly keep up. "Come on, Booger, you know you can't bring a girl in our room, then your imaginary girl would have to get kicked out of your dreams. You don't want that, do you?"

Smiles are everywhere as they guys eat. I see a couple of them thinking, sly smiles are beginning to form. I'm in trouble. I already like these guys.

Jimmy is sitting across from me. He's smiling. He tugs on his rosary beads draped around his neck as he looks around the room. He leans in over the table, "Hey, which one of these mommas have you invited into our cabin, John? Huh? Huh!" The whole table erupts.

"Oh sh*t, homie!" Booger says.

I smack him on the back of his head, "That's another rule. We can't say cuss words."

Lonny was one step ahead of me. He raises his hand and speaks confidently, "What do you consider a cuss word, Counselor John? Obviously, 'Sh*t.' What else? Do you consider the word 'F...'"

"Stop!" I put one finger up. "Stop." He stops as the whole table falls out. Lonny high fives Booger. Jimmy daps the kid next to him. The girls at the next table are watching. Beth shakes her head and gives me the "get it together" look. I look at the boys and laugh, shaking my head in surrender.

18.

We've had an absolute blast the last couple of days playing basketball, swimming. We even spent a bunch of time doing arts & crafts, Booger is an amazing artist! The skits during tonight's campfire have been hilarious. Even the singing has been fun. By the time Pastor Wes gets up to talk he has our total attention. The whole day has moved us to this point. I look down to confirm my thinking. Yep, every single one of my guys is tuned in as Pastor Wes flips a few pages in his Bible.

"I want to ask you three questions tonight. That's all. So, this talk is going to be short." A few kids cheer. Lonny and Booger are sitting next to me. They're both intently listening.

"Question #1: Where are you? Question #2: Who told you that? Question #3: What have you done?'"

And then he sits down. Startled, I looked around. Will smiles and daps one the kid sitting next to him. It was like a mini-celebration that the sermon was over. Davis and I used to do it after every Sunday sermon.

Mrs. Johnson gets up, "Let's talk about these questions more this week. Is that okay?" Everyone nods and agrees, although unsure of what is going to happen next.

Mrs. Johnson asks Pete and Beth to come and join her in leading some songs. We sing some of the silliest songs while doing crazy motions. It's cool to see Mrs. Johnson fully animated, especially after these semi-serious questions.

We eventually head back to the cabins. Lonny and Booger are walking together ahead of me, talking about Pastor Wes. Booger's got his hands in his pockets and the coolest strut. He leans in toward Lonny, "What's up with the priest homie?"

"I don't know. He seems alright. I don't think he's a priest though. I don't know what he is. Shortest sermon I've ever heard. Way better than our priest." He pauses and then says, "What about those questions though. Kinda deep…"

Booger leans in a bit more, "Nada. All I know is I'm at camp, ese. And this place is full of beautiful mommas. I'm hoping to do something with them. I know that answer."

19.

The cabin is finally quiet. These guys have totally drawn me in and worn me out. I can't figure out if they're innocent or if they're filling me with lies. There isn't one of them who isn't totally here. I see that. I feel that. They're fully present. I love that.

I'm sitting by the window, reading *The Magician's Nephew* aloud, as Will opens the door and quietly steps into the dark room. "Elton John. Let's go," he loudly whispers.

Lonny rolls over and then leans up from his bed, "Counselor John, why is Counselor Will in here? He's not supposed to be in here…unless you're gay. Are you gay Counselor John? Is that why he called you Elton John? Elton John is gay for sure." The boys who are still awake are now laughing. I get up and walk across the room toward Will.

Will looks over at Lonny and whispers, "What's up with this kid?"

"He's fine. He's messing with you. He's quickly become my favorite person ever."

"Whatever. You ready? Let's go."

"Hold on. Give me a few minutes so I can be sure this crew is asleep and then I'll come up and meet you at the picnic table."

"Alright. Hurry up."

I glance out the window and see Pete and Mark are at the table. The picnic table has become our after-curfew spot.

I read a couple more chapters, laughing at the end of chapter seven. I stick the old photograph I use as a bookmark in place and push back the stool. Glancing out the window I see Will setting down a stuffed brown paper bag. After curfew, me or Will usually run down and break into the canteen for late night snacks. I throw my book on the bed in my room and make my way to the door.

Lonny rolls over. "You going to see your girl, Counselor John?"

"No, Lonny. I'm going down to the picnic table…what girl?"

"Whatever, Counselor John. You know you're in love with Counselor Laney. I've seen you staring at her."

"Get out of here, homie. Go back to sleep and keep dreaming about one day meeting a girl as beautiful as Counselor Laney."

He points his finger at me like a gun. "Gotcha Counselor John." He laughs a very tired laugh. His eyes look a different kind of tired.

I stop and sit at the bottom of his bed. "Hey, you know I'm not going anywhere right? I'm here with you. You know that, right?"

"I know. I can tell." He slowly rolls over away from me. "You are the only

one."
            "Nah. I don't believe that…you want to talk about it?"
            "Nada, go make out your boyfriends."
            I pat him on his leg. "Alright, dude. I'm around when you're up for it."

20.

Over the next couple of days, I try to stay in step with Lonny. We talk for a few minutes at the pool. He tells me about a slow rotation of his mom's boyfriends and stepdads coming through the kitchen. Our conversation is intense and he starts to tear up a few times. I try to honor him by giving him some space, but as soon as I do, I lose him. He jumps in the pool and doesn't come out until the whistle blows. I track him down at free time and try to step back in. I can tell he wants to talk but as soon as Booger and Jimmy come over he shuts down. I try everything I can to get those two to leave, even offering to buy them something from the canteen. But they don't want to leave. I figure they just want to be with Lonny. Booger might think he is their leader, but Lonny is the one they follow.

There is something about Lonny that keeps pulling me toward him…it's Davis, I think. Lonny reminds me a lot of Davis. That must be it. Or maybe he reminds me of me. Oh, God no.

After missing Davis for the last couple of days I decide to try him again. Finally, he picks up. I'm so glad to hear his voice instead of the annoying answering machine.

"Hey, lil' bro. How are you? What's going on?"

"I'm good, Big. Mom is fine. I don't know what happened the other night, but you know how she does. She's pretending like it never happened."

"Dang, that means it was a big deal."

"For sure. You know it was."

"You okay, Davis? We talked about me coming home. You need me to come home?"

"Nah, I got it, bro. You do your thing. Tell me about camp. What's going on there?"

"Man, there is this girl here. I'm totally into her. I think she's starting to figure it out."

"Oh, that's cool. Hey, Big, Dawn's been asking me about you. She grabbed me yesterday and goes, 'I know you talk to your brother all the time. Next time you talk to him, tell him I'd like to hear from him too.'"

"Ah, Dawn's cool. I'll call her sometime soon. Listen, you don't have to cover for me. Not now, not ever. You do your thing."

"For sure, Big."

"How about Pops? Is he okay?"

"I haven't seen him much. He and his new wife are out all the time. It's good to hear him laugh. I forgot how dorky his laugh is. It's so embarrassing."

Now we both laugh. "I've missed that laugh too. Guess she's good for him then. Miss your laugh too, Davis. There's this kid out here who reminds me of you. He's the coolest kid ever."

"Dude, that's fresh."

"And I want you to meet this girl sometime. I'll need to meet her first, but, you know!"

"Cool, take a picture or just bring her home at the end of the summer. We'll take her to Disneyland, show her the way we do things."

"Sounds good, man. I'd love that." I find myself smiling as I think about it.

"Me too. Gotta run, Big. Going to meet some guys before tonight's practice. Love you, Big!"

"Love you, too, Davis."

21.

Night falls. I meet the guys at the picnic table. Mark's in the middle of talking about how he's falling for Phoebe. "She's even teaching me some phrases in Spanish."

I glance at Will and in unison we say, "Vista, she's quite a view."

"You two are idiots," Mark says as he laughs at us.

Pete says he's beyond falling for Beth. "I'm in deep." We nod in agreement. It's been obvious since the first day of the summer.

"Will, what about you and Marcie?" Mark asks.

"I don't know, dude. I like her and all, but I don't like her the way Pete likes Beth. Sometimes I feel like I'm using her." He stops strumming. He stops us.

A few moments later Pete asks, "How do you know the difference between lust and love?"

Mark looks upward as he thinks about his response. "I don't know exactly. I think at first it is lust, combined with like a 'love at first sight' thing. And then it moves to less lust and more love."

"How does that work?" I ask. "Now you only have like 40 percent lust and 60 percent is love?"

"I don't think I've ever thought about a girl where lust hasn't at least been a part of the equation," Pete says.

Will starts strumming again, "I guess it's love if you've gotten what you've lusted for and you still want to hang around."

"That sort of makes sense to me," I say. "But even after I've gotten what I want, why do I still want more?"

Will points at me with his guitar pick. "What if you lust and love and never act out on it all? Because that's you, Dr. John. At some point, you're going to have to act on either your lust or your love for Ivy League."

"Come on now, I'm trying something different. I'm trying to play it smooth!"

Will glides his fingertips over the wood of his guitar. "You're the epitome of smooth. Keep telling yourself that."

We are laughing and carrying on, oblivious to the fact that the whole world is asleep, when a flashlight shines right on us. We cover our eyes, not sure whether to make a run for it or raise our hands in surrender. The light clicks off and we hear laughter.

"Hey, Choir Boys. Whatcha doing out so far past curfew?" We all are totally relieved and totally freaked out as Sandy and Joanna emerge from the darkness.

The light clicks on and off again. They laugh a little louder as Will jumps from the table and tries to both celebrate and soften their arrival.

"Hey girls," Mark whispers.

I get up to hug Joanna. She's wearing my sweatshirt. She kisses me before I can get to the hug. "Well hello to you too," I say.

"Hey Mark. Hey Pete's Dragon. Hey there John," Sandy says, with Will leading her to the table, his arm slung around her shoulder and his smile as big as the moon.

"What are you guys doing out here?" I whisper as both girls sit between Will and me on the bench.

Joanna looks me in the eyes. "It's Wednesday."

"Oh, right. So sorry."

"We'll forgive you for not coming out to our campout," Sandy says. "But once our girls went to sleep we thought we'd come surprise you guys. Can't believe you're still up. It's like 1:30 in the morning!"

"This is one of my favorite times of the day," Pete says. "I love it when we get to hang out like this."

Sandy pokes Pete, "Ah, that's sweet Pete," She laughs out loud, "'Sweet Pete.' That's a better nickname. That suits you!" We fill the next minutes with different variations of 'Sweet Pete' jokes.

Joanna leans her head on my shoulder. I can smell pot on her skin and a hint of alcohol on her breath. It becomes a mix of desire and homesickness. I haven't felt this way since I left Dawn at the party after the last day at school. I am transfixed.

Sandy surveys the table and then looks at Will. "So, what are you guys talking about so late?"

"We were talking about lust and love. What else?" Will says.

"You silly boys. That's what you always talk about," she says.

"What do girls talk about this late?" Mark asks.

"Girls talk about the same thing, lust and love. What else would we talk about?"

Joanna slips her hand on my thigh and rubs her thumb up and down.

"That settles it," Will determines. "Lust and love for everyone." He smiles at Sandy. She kisses him.

I rest my hand on Joanna's hand. "Hey, let us walk you back to your campsite. We don't want these guys to get jealous."

Joanna looks directly into my eyes as if I'm the only one at the table. I know the look. I stare back at her. She says, "Another walk in the dark sounds good to me." I'm in a free fall.

Will and Sandy get up from the table. Pete and Mark start putting the board game away.

"Hey, Mark, for the record, I was winning that game, make sure you write down the score," Will says.

"Of course you were, Wild Willy," Sandy says. She whispers something into Will's ear. He laughs and pulls out the ponytail in his hair. Sandy shakes Wills long hair as they begin to walk down the dark dirt road.

Joanna and I get up to follow.

"Good night, guys," Joanna says to Mark and Pete. She looks at me, waving her flashlight, "Let's go."

I look back at the guys and then at Joanna. I slip my hand in her hand, our fingers lace. She leans in closer. I inhale…and then exhale as we walk quietly into the darkness.

22.

I read somewhere, "arousal gives birth to shame and shame gives birth to arousal." It's a twisted cycle. I know it well. Damn.

I have no idea how I got here or how to get out of here. I just know I'm here. There's a part of me that is so disgusted at being here again and there's another part of me that revels in the despair.

23.

Pastor Wes takes his usual place in front of the campfire. I've avoided looking at him all day. I can't look at him now. Not after last night. He starts telling the Creation story. He invites all of us to say, "And it was good." I play along. Lonny sits next to me. He's having a blast nudging me each time, "And it was good!"

I know where Pastor Wes is going. I knew it from the moment he started. I mouthed the words along with him, "And they were naked and felt no shame." What the hell…

He went on about the pain of guilt and shame. I was somewhat hopeful for something new, but he repeated the same tired mantra. I don't need it repeated. It's tattooed on my soul.

He finally moves on to what happens in the story. Adam and Eve eat the apple. "And they realize they are naked and everything goes to hell."

Shock and gasps fill the air. Lonny whispers something to Booger. They go back and forth, and then Booger leans over him and says to me, "This is NOT the way our priest tells the story, ese." Jimmy nervously puts his rosary beads in his mouth, never taking his eyes off Pastor Wes.

"I told you guys, sometimes Pastor Wes tells the story differently. He puts himself in the story, remember?"

As if on cue Pastor Wes says, *"Wes, where are you?'* I heard God say. *'Wes, where are you?'"*

Pastor Wes wipes his face for dramatic effect. He almost whispers. "I'm hiding, God. Don't come here. I don't want you to see me like this."

"You're naked. Aren't you Wes?"

"Yes."

Pastor Wes slowly moves forward and addresses us, "Where do you go when you hide?"

The younger kids are clearly lost, but every single one of my guys is totally fixated. "Tell the person sitting next to you where you go when you hide."

It's quiet for a moment as kids aren't sure if they're supposed to actually answer. I tap Lonny on the leg. "What's up homie? Where do you go?"

"Vamanos, Counselor John. You first."

"I'm the counselor so you get to go first."

He takes a quick glance over his shoulder. "My mom's new boyfriend has these magazines. I guess I hide there. Now you."

"I get it. I've hidden there too. Sometimes still do." He doesn't flinch. His eyes are locked on mine. I nod, keeping my eyes on his. "I go radio silent I guess. I don't, like, run away. I fade behind the smile. I can be in a room full of people and be totally hidden."

"Whoa. That's deep, Counselor John."

Pastor Wes interrupts with a shout of audacity. *"Who told you that, Wes?"* he says with great conviction. *"Who told that you were naked?"* He says it again, even stronger, *"Who told you that? Wes?"* Silence follows. A long, deep silence. *"It wasn't me!"* He says just as strongly. *"I didn't tell you that. I didn't tell you were naked. Who have you been listening to?"*

I look over at Laney. It's the first time I've managed to look at her all day and all night. I know where she's sitting. I know what's she's wearing. I know how she's doing, but I couldn't bring myself to look at her; now I can't look away. Her face is strong and her eyes soft. She's very slowly braiding the hair of a girl sitting in front of her.

Pastor Wes comes back to us and speaks to us again, "Who told you that? Who told you that you were too fat or too dumb or too slow or too ugly or too broken or too sinful? Who told you that? It wasn't God!" He matches his previous conviction, "It wasn't God!"

He moves back and says softly, *"What have you done, Wes? What have you done?"* He looks back at us and then looks down. "What have you done? What have you done that's so bad, that God can't forgive?" He waits for the stillness to settle. "Nothing."

He looks back at us again. He speaks softly and pastorally, "1. Where are you, where do you go when you hide? 2. Who told you that? What voices are you listening to? 3. What have you done that you believe is too much for God to forgive?" He walks out of the campfire pit and onto the dirt road.

"Damn," Lonny says with extreme seriousness in his eyes. "That's way deeper than you, Counselor John." I nod. That's all I can do. Nod. I can't speak.

I have no words.

24.

The guys are getting into bed as I go through the motions, looking for my long sleeve flannel in my tiny closet. I'm awakened from my stupor by Lonny standing in the doorway. He doesn't say anything. He's just standing there. He has his hands in his pockets and for some reason he's wearing Jimmy's rosary beads.

While going through my pile of clothes, I catch him looking over his shoulder out into the cabin and then back at me. He begins to speak softly, slowly, and deliberately. "What if it wasn't something you've done? What if it was something done to you?" He leans up against the door jam. The look on his face instantly sucks the life out of me.

I pull out my flannel. I have one-eighth of a second to think of what to say and realize I don't even need that much time. God I know his pain. I can't ever forget it. I can feel it, even now. I look him in the eyes. "I am sorry, Lonny. I am so sorry." I sit on my bed and he falls onto it next to me. I slip my arm around him and hug him. His pain stirring him. I say it again touching his arm, "I'm so sorry, Lonny." Tears begin to stream down his face. The rest of his body is paralyzed. I say it again, "I'm so sorry, Lonny. I'm so sorry." Then he breaks.

I don't say anything. I know not to. I just hold him. Soon enough I begin to wipe my face. All of this in Lonny somehow cracks something long calloused within me. It's a deeper shame being unearthed. "I'm so sorry," I say. I don't know if I'm speaking to Lonny, or Joanna, or Davis, or to God.

Tears begin to form in my eyes. I squeeze my eyes closed as if to cut off the pain that is flowing all over me. When I open my eyes, I see Jimmy now kneeling in front of Lonny. Tears are running down his face. Booger is standing right behind him. A few of the other guys are now standing guard too. A couple guys are crying because their leader is hurting. Lonny looks up and sees them and goes back to sobbing.

The front door open and then closes. I assume one of my guys is making a run for it. I've learned these kids either are drawn to intimacy or freaked out by it. I'm about to send someone out to rescue my wounded camper when Pastor Wes looks over the guys at me. I'm startled to see him. I wait for him to come through the huddle of boys to help me. He just stands there behind them, looking around at the boys and then glancing back at me and Lonny. He nods at me and then closes his eyes and tilts his head back. He pushes up the sleeves of his sweatshirt and stretches his hands over my guys. Lonny begins to settle down. I whisper, "I'm so sorry. I'm so sorry." I rock with him for a few moments. I look up again, certain Pastor Wes is going to do something. He stands silent for a few moments, looking over all that is happening. He puts his hands together in front of his slightly smiling face and slowly nods at me. Then turns back toward the door. I'm left alone in all of this hurt. All of it.

Lonny takes a few deep breaths. He's beginning to settle down a little more. Outwardly, he's almost quiet.

"You guys get back to bed," I say to the boys crowded in the doorway. "Say a prayer for your boy…for all of us." Lonny wipes his face with his dirty white T-shirt. Most of the guys head back to their beds. Jimmy and Booger don't move. I catch Lonny's eyes before he hangs his head again. "You okay, Lonny?"

He shakes his head. He wants to speak but can't. He looks up at me and tries to smile. I hold him tighter and say, "Hey, man. It's cool. I've got you. You're safe here, you know?"

We are quiet, save the occasional gasp in trying to catch our breath. In this moment, more than any other moment, there is a peace. There is a raging war being fought right here for this kid's soul, and there is a peace – a weird, sweet, calming, gentle quietness that holds the four of us completely together.

Lonny runs his fingers over the rosary beads and whispers, "It's hell Counselor John."

Booger speaks for the first time. He looks so respectfully at Lonny and asks, "What's hell, ese?"

I look at Booger. His eyes are so full of tenderness and compassion. Tears begin running down his face. He wants desperately to understand. He kneels down next to Jimmy. Jimmy feels Booger's presence in a new way and his tears start again. Lonny leans back, now fully against the wall. He looks at me and then looks away closing his eyes, trying to hold back the tears that come anyway.

"It is hell, Lonny," I say. He wipes these new tears with his sleeve. He slowly looks up at me. I nod, "I used to think hell was this place where all the bad people go when they die, you know?" He almost smiles. "That's not hell. Red devil running around like the Arizona State mascot, pitchfork in his hand, poking people, fire burning all over the place. That's not hell."

Booger nods in an uncertain agreement. Lonny is listening to me like I've never been listened to before. My tears now match Jimmy's. I let them come without wiping them away. "This is hell, it's innocence brutally taken. Hell is being broken, never to be whole again. Hell is being used and thrown away like a piece of trash. Hell is being told, 'It's our little secret and if you tell anyone, I'll hurt your little brother too.' That's hell. It's the loneliest place on earth."

Lonny bursts into tears and falls into my arms. The other two boys now feeling the heaviness of the weight of his pain, mine too. They envelop us with their tears. Our cries fill the empty sky.

25.

There's a peace at the breakfast table. It's the peace birthed by brokenness. We pass the pancakes and syrup like monks in a monastery. I keep an eye on Lonny. He's stoic. I wonder if he's having buyer's remorse. I remember doing the whole altar call confession one time at church. I was confessing about being with this girl. All these adults were around me, patting me on my back as I confessed, and my mom looking at me in complete disgust. God, I hate that look. As soon as I got up from the altar, I regretted sharing the whole story, more than the story itself.

Booger breaks our liturgy of silent prayer. "What happens in this family stays in this family. We don't need to be talking about last night with other people. We are family, homies." The boys respond in great respect. He points his knife across the table, "And because we are family, I want to remind you that you need a date to tonight's Moonlight Hike. I'm taking Vanessa. I can't help most of you dateless fools. But for $10, I'll hook you up."

Conversation starts about the hike, and within moments, most of the heaviness is lifted. For the first time, I look for Laney. Really look for her. As I scan the room, I see Pastor Wes and Andee talking in the corner. Their faces stone me as they look at me and my guys and then at each other and then back at us. I know the look. They're plotting a fix for something that can't be fixed.

I get up from the table and lean over it, "Booger, each of these guys need a date. Figure it out." I turn around and walk toward Pastor Wes and Andee.

Andee points toward my table as I approach her, "You need to stay with your campers, John."

"I'm with them. They know I'm with them." I look at Pastor Wes, "Are you talking about last night?"

"Yes, I was telling Andee how proud of you I am. You handled that situation with such grace."

"Thanks. What else?"

Andee quickly speaks first, "John, if the camper confessed to something I'll need to write a report on him. Did he confess to something? I know you are good at hearing confessions."

I'm incredulous, "What the…" I stop myself. "Did he confess? What are you talking about? You don't even know what you're talking about!"

Pastor Wes rests his hand on my shoulder, "We trust you, John. We only want to make sure we support him in every way possible."

Andee says bluntly, "What did he do, John?"

"He didn't do anything. God!"

"Well why was he so emotional then?" Andee says.

"Because he's a kid. He has a real heart with a real hurt. And the truth is he didn't say what happened, and I'm not going to ask him. It's his story to tell. It's his story to live!" I look at Andee. "Please don't make him another one of your pet projects, Andee. And Pastor Wes, if you wanted to help, why didn't you do it last night?"

"I did do something, John. I entrusted him to you," Pastor Wes says.

Andee rolls her eyes, "Listen, we are only trying to help the boy."

"The boy has a name. It's Lonny. And I know you're trying to help, but standing over here in the corner plotting about all the ways you can fix him is not helping him. Stop trying to fix him. He'll be okay."

Andee coils up even more tightly while Pastor Wes begins to soften. "John," he says, "Please let us know how we can help."

"Please leave him be. Please. He's a great kid. He's okay. He'll be okay." I turn around before Andee can say anything else and come back to the table. It's now regained its silence. I look around at their hung heads. Only Lonny looks up at me. He tries to smile but can't.

26.

I've scrambled all day and have dates for most of the guys in my cabin. Booger and Vanessa matched Lonny up with another girl from Beth's cabin. Lonny's excited. Life has returned to him. He's now in total control. His wit has somehow reached a new high…or low. I'm out of breath trying to keep up.

Pastor Wes asks Mark and Vista to lead the Hike. They stand in front of us, joined by Pete and Beth. I look for Laney. I'm assuming Danny will be her date tonight.

Booger strolls down the dirt path with Vanessa on his arm. It's like he's on the red carpet at Mann's Chinese Theater down on Hollywood Boulevard. He's stoked. Hair slicked back under his tight net, clean white shirt, denim Dickie's jacket and matching pants. He is practically perfect. Lonny struts behind, his girl at his side. Lonny's got one hand in his Dickie's, the other arm swinging big, up and back, in cadence with his girl. He's wearing my flannel with the top button buttoned over his white t-shirt.

I spot Laney coming with a small group of girls. She's attached to a girl on either hand. I look for Danny, but he's MIA. I move toward her but then stop. The thoughts of the other night with Joanna play in my mind. Guilt and shame, my two lifelong companions, remind me I don't have the right to even look at her. I turn away as a couple of boys from Pete's cabin come by me and high five. We joke around about being dateless.

I hear Laney stop behind us. Her voice alone soothes me.

One of her girls calls out to me, "Hey John."

I spin around and say, "Hey girls, how are we all tonight?"

They smile and giggle. The boys behind me have now joined me at my side. Lined up across from each other, we look like we are about to either have a square dance or a gang fight.

"These guys next to me are looking for dates. You girls are way too beautiful for these homies, so I wouldn't ask you to go on a 'date' with them, but how about we all do the Hike together?"

Laney smiles and joins me, "What do you think girls? Do these guys look trustworthy to you?" They giggle and nod approvingly. "I can't vouch for all of these boys, but I think the big kid is trustworthy."

The girls look back at her, "Let's walk with them!" Laney nods at them and then looks back at us.

"Let's do it then. This will be epic!" I declare. Laney smiles my way.

The boys and girls begin to mingle as I scramble for something to say to Laney.

"How are things, John?"

"Things are good. We've had a pretty intense last few days, but good. What about you? How are you?"

"I'm good. I've fallen in love with just about every girl in my cabin."

"That's awesome. There's a couple guys in my cabin who won't be easy to forget." I point over to Booger and Lonny. "You see those two guys. I'd give about anything for those guys."

"Aw, I'm so glad, John."

"I can't believe they're leaving tomorrow. I'm honestly going to miss those guys."

She smiles and places her hand on my arm, "Y'all have had a great time together, I've noticed."

Wait, what did she just say? She's "noticed?" I want so much to talk with her, to really talk with her, about all of it. I scramble for the right words, looking past her, looking down, then finally looking in her eyes. I can't do it. Instead, I blurt out, "How have you been spending your free time? You reading anything good?" I cringe inside with disbelief. God.

"Not too much. I'm supposed to be reading *Crime and Punishment* for a summer class." She laughs. "I started it on the plane ride out here. I'm still not even half-way."

"I know the book," I say. I decide to let the other stuff go and just go with this conversation. I smile and try to enter in. "Dostoyevsky is one of my dad's favorites. He's got a big library at home and Dostoyevsky fills it. His all-time favorite line is, 'Beauty will save the world.'"

She looks at me as if she's found something. She does this gorgeous thing raising one eyebrow. "Really? Wow. Have you read much of his work?"

"I actually started *The Brothers Karamazov* this spring but got sidetracked. What about you? Sounds like you read a lot. Do you write too?"

"No. I'm not a writer. I do admire the way some people can express themselves through writing." She stops and hugs a girl who has run up to her. She holds her tight. "You like to write, don't you John? Have you been writing anything lately?" She smiles at the girl, and the girl runs off.

"Um…not much, I've started a piece a couple of times."

"Oh, really? Tell me about it."

"It's nothing, sort of a 'Holden Caulfield goes to camp.' I can't pull it together. I keep getting distracted."

"Oh, wow. Can't wait to read it. *Catcher in the Rye* is one of my all-time favorites. What's the phrase? She smiles and nods her head, "Wait, wait…'*What really knocks me out is a book that, when you're done reading it, you wish the author that wrote it was a terrific friend of yours and you could call him up on the phone whenever you felt like it. That doesn't happen much, though.*'" She smiles the biggest smile.

"Oh, my God. Are you kidding me? That's so freaking awesome. You're absolutely amazing!" I try and regain my composure. "And for the record J.D. Salinger is definitely a guy!" She laughs her most elegant laugh. And then the moment closes. From nowhere, Danny appears. He has no problem interrupting the greatest three minutes of my life.

"May I have this dance?" he says, as he takes off his sun visor and bows in front of Laney.

"That's kind, Danny. Thank you. But my girls and I are committed to this handsome bunch of boys."

Danny deflates internally. I can see it. I don't think Laney sees it, but he's gasping for air. I'm praying he drowns. He looks over his shoulder and then back toward her, "Listen, I've got to check with Andee about one more detail for tonight, and then I'll circle back. See you in a few." He looks my way but not at me. He wouldn't dare let Laney see him get snarky as he crawls away.

The loudspeaker goes off, and we all start to move up the dirt road. Kids are running back and forth as the sun begins to set. I keep watch over Lonny and Booger. They look like they're having the finest night of their lives. I smile and look over as Laney talks with some girls behind her. This might be the finest night of my life.

She and I walk together, but we don't really talk to each other. We keep the conversation going with the kids, ensuring they're having fun. The closest I get to Laney all night is a kind smile at the end of the hike. I've never been excited by ending the night with a smile in my life!

"Thanks, John. This was fun."

My guys pose and posture and smack each other and blow kisses as the girls turn toward their cabin. We turn back and head toward our cabin. My guys all fall into bed, totally spent, and totally full. They have found freedom here.

<h1 style="text-align:center">27.</h1>

I scribble my address on the inside of one of the camp Bibles and hand it to Lonny. He has already written his address and phone number on a piece of folded notebook paper and hands it to me. "Here," he says. "You can write me a letter if you want."

I throw my arm around him. "I still got you, homie," I say as we walk toward the bus. Lonny holds a black plastic bag full of dirty clothes in one hand and an empty suitcase, save one camp Bible, in the other.

"I know you do. Thanks, Counselor John." He smiles and then tears up. "I'm going to talk to someone when I get home."

"That's the best news ever. I'm super proud of you, Lonny. Secrets suck. I know that much. It won't get better staying inside. It will only get heavier. That I know."

"I know you're right. I'll keep in touch."

"Hey, I love you, Lonny. You know that?"

"I know you do, Counselor John. It feels good." He turns toward the bus. Andee is checking kids off the list on her clipboard as they come to the bottom step.

I watch, standing guard, ready to step in if needed.

"Name?" She calls out without looking up.

"Lonny Diaz."

She looks up and sees him, and then she sees me, and then looks at him, and then down at her paper.

He turns back toward me, "Adios, Counselor John. Hope Counselor Laney falls in love with you." He laughs at himself. I laugh at him and shake my head.

Andee sighs and mumbles something under her breath. She bends down and pulls a camp Bible out of the box next to her, "Here's a Bible." She opens up the front flap. "Here's our address and phone number. Please give me your phone number so I can follow up with you."

"Oh, thank you, but I don't need the Bible." He looks back over his shoulder and motions, "Counselor John already gave me one, and he has my phone number too." He steps into the bus. Booger gives me the biggest bear hug of my life. He checks in next and then hops on the bus with the rest of the guys. Jimmy is last. He takes off his rosary beads and places them over my head.

"No way, dude. These are yours."

"I want you to have them. Those are important to me. I want you and this camp to have them. God's done answered my prayers, ese. Wear these. Maybe He'll answer yours too."

We hug again and Jimmy goes up the stairs of the bus as Pete jumps off after loading a few things for the driver. His face lights up as he points to the necklace, "Did your boys give you those rosary beads? That's big, dude. That's really big."

Andee is straining to listen as we walk away.

"No kidding. Maybe God will answer my prayers about Laney if I wear these."

He smiles his big smile, "Not even rosary beads can you help you there, man."

We walk toward the cabins. I seriously want to tell Pete about the other night. I want to ask him about prayer. I want to ask him about his prayer. I want to know why God didn't do anything when all that sh*t was going down with Lonny, with me. I prayed and prayed and prayed and nothing. Why didn't God do something? Anything?

Pete interrupts my descent into oblivion, "Dude, what a great time. That was so awesome." The buses honk as they slowly drive over the ridge.

28.

Andee scowls and motions for us to sit in the far corner as we walk in late to the staff meeting. We cross the room in true Abbey-Road fashion. There's a spot next to Laney and the guys leave the space for me to slide in next to her.

"Hey," I whisper. "Last night was great."

She acknowledges me with a smile but doesn't answer. Her silence makes me nervous. Andee begins reviewing statistics from our last camp.

"Fifty-seven campers made first-time decisions for Christ." The staff applaud loudly.

She continues, "Eighty-one campers recommitted their lives for Christ." Same enthusiasm.

"And one staff member was fired."

A deafening silence overtakes everything good. It's a sound too familiar to me. Everyone looks around to see who is missing. I drop my head.

Andee doesn't skip a beat, "I fired Chris who worked in the kitchen. He wasn't choosing the right things. Let's learn from this. Learn what not to choose."

I don't really know Chris, hardly at all, but I'm certain I know his choices.

Pastor Wes steps in, "Listen, I know you guys are tired. You've worked hard. Thanks for giving it your all." He rubs his hands through his hair. "I'm learning that sin looks most attractive when I'm tired, bored, or lonely." Heads nod around the room, including Laney's. I decide to step out again and whisper toward her, "That's me for sure."

She looks directly at me as if to look inside of me. "You too?" she whispers. She doesn't smile, but there is something in her eyes. I stare back at her. She just let me see something inside her that isn't visible to the rest of the world.

"Rest and celebrate these next few days, family," Pastor Wes says. He looks over at Mrs. Johnson. She looks excited. Really excited.

Mrs. Johnson closes her Bible on her lap and says, "One more thing before you go. I've bought a bunch of passes to Big Surf for tomorrow. It just so happens to be Christian Music day at the park, and some Christian musicians are playing all day long. I know you're tired, but this might be a great way to relax and be encouraged."

Pastor Wes adds, "We've even bought some meet and greet passes for the last band of the night. We think you'll have a great time if you choose to come. No pressure, just an invitation. You're dismissed."

Mrs. Johnson immediately starts handing out the tickets. I hear Elton John in my head, *Jesus freaks / Out in the streets / Handing tickets out for God.*

I look at the guys. Will's shaking his head. I can tell he wants to stick with our plan to go camping. I can also tell the other guys are hedging. I lean over to

Laney to try and keep whatever connection we had a moment ago.

"So, what are you plans for the break?"

"I'm not sure. A few of us had planned to hang around here today, and then go into Tucson tomorrow for Mexican food and a movie."

"Sounds like a good day."

"I guess you guys will be going to the Surf place?"

"We actually talked about going camping and doing some cliff diving in the Salt River, but I'd imagine those guys might want to go to the concert. What about you, you think you'll come up for the concert?"

"I'm not much of a water park girl, and I don't know much Christian music."

"Big Surf is a pretty awesome spot. It's got a great beach where you can hang out and relax. You could lay up on the beach and read. I'm not much of Christian music guy either, but maybe we can check it out together."

She smiles and leans back, "Maybe. Let me know if you guys decide to go."

I try to play it smooth, but I'm so freaking stoked!

Laney and I stand and we're immediately face-to-face with Danny. He turns and pulls in Crafty, Andee, Bernice and some others. They all circle up. Will's waving at me. I look to acknowledge him while holding my breath. I stand in between the two groups.

Danny says, "You guys want to go to Big Surf tomorrow? Sounds like fun with the water park and everything."

Laney listens as everyone else answers. I wait for her response. Then she says, "I'm not sure. We'll see."

Danny steps toward her. "Let me know," he says. "I'd really like to spend the day with you."

I know I'm not included in this conversation, but I hear every word. My ears examine every intonation; my eyes monitor every wink and wrinkle, every slight movement of the head.

"Well, thanks. I'm sure I'd enjoy that, but no promises," Laney says.

Will grabs my arm and pulls me over and turns us all together. "Listen, Christian music sucks. I've been to these Christian nights before. They always suck. The bands are terrible – they're such wannabes. Guys, let's skip the concert and stay out at the river."

Pete is smiling and laughs a little. "Come on, Will. The Christian bands can't be that bad, plus Big Surf is fun."

Mark agrees with Pete, "Why don't we camp out tonight and do the Big Surf thing tomorrow? We can go back out to the campsite after the concert, or we can crash at Ms. Audrey's house."

Will's frustration is beginning to show, "Come on guys, let's go camping." He looks at me for support as I look back at Laney.

Mark steps in to mediate, "I think we campout tonight and then decide. Maybe we go and check out the concert. I think it would mean a lot to Pastor Wes if we show up."

"Oh, God. Who freaking cares?" Will says throwing up his arms. He sighs and backs off just a little. "Guys, come on, this is our only long break of the summer. I don't want to spend it with the whole staff. Let's just stick with the plan."

Because of the Laney conversation, there's no way I'm not showing at Big Surf. "Look, man. These guys are so whipped that they want to be with their girls, and if they aren't with them they're going to be whining the whole time. Let's compromise and go up to the concert tomorrow night."

"You can't be serious! God!"

Pastor Wes and Mrs. Johnson are talking up the Big Surf event in the parking lot as Will and I jump in my truck.

Pastor Wes motions toward us and we slow to a stop. Will winds down the window to talk with him. I look back and see Laney. I wave and she waves back and walks toward us.

She stops next to the window, her hands resting loosely in her pockets and says, "Hey you."

"Hey, you. You heading out for Mexican food and a movie?"

She pulls up her Wayfarers to hold her hair back and leans down a little.

"We are. We decided to go into Tucson for the evening." She smiles the most beautiful smile I've ever seen. I'm sure the people on the other side of the canyon can see the beams coming from my face as I smile. She catches me looking and slowly looks down with a huge smile. She looks up again and says, "What did you guys decide about the concert?"

I glance toward Will, "We are going to campout tonight and then decide."

Will, who is in this conversation with Pastor Wes, is totally aware of what's going on in my conversation with Laney. He leans over me to talk with Laney, "Why don't you guys meet us there? Maybe we all can hang out at the concert."

Laney looks at me and then across at Will, "We'll see. That would be fun." She looks back at me. "Save me seat, just in case, okay?" She squeezes my arm and walks away. Pastor Wes high five's Will and then turns to speak with someone else.

Will and I wind up our windows without saying a word.

Once the windows are up, he yells, "Save me a seat!" He shakes his head and gets louder. "What just happened? She basically just said she was ready to have your children!"

I don't say a word. I can't. My smile prevents my mouth from moving. We stop one last time by the cabins to grab our sleeping bags and backpacks. I run into my cabin and grab my stuff. My Bible and notebook are on the windowsill and catch my eye. I grab them both, thinking I need all the luck I can get. I almost grab the rosary beads but know I'm getting kinda crazy.

As I run back to the truck, Will is talking with Mark and Pete. Mark, leaning on his bumper yells, "Dude, Ivy League! Will just told us you guys are getting married!"

Will won't relent. Every few minutes he shakes his head and says, "You have no chance with her, you know that, right?"

I keep trying to change the subject or just enjoy my fleeting moment, and he keeps bringing me back to reality. "You have absolutely no chance on this planet to date Ivy League."

I laugh and turn up the music. Dire Straits' *Sultans of Swing* starts playing. I turn it up again. Will grabs his guitar and begins to play along. I bang out the drum solo on the steering wheel, letting out a load roar at the end. Will laughs and shakes his head, "You're a mess, dude. A total mess. I'm happy for you. You know that right?"

"I know. I do."

We drive quietly for a while and then he looks over one last time and says, "You still have no shot. She's Ivy League!"

<h1 style="text-align:center">30.</h1>

We are sunburned after tubing and cliff diving all day. The cool of the late night feels good on my skin.

"Check it out. A waxing crescent?" Mark says, pointing to the moon.

"Is that really what it's called? You could be making this stuff up for all we know," Will says. He strums a few chords and finger picks. "I can't figure it out."

"Figure out what, Will?" Mark asks.

"The perfect song for this moment." He strums and picks a note and then swears. He tries again. "I can't get it." He gets up and starts walking around, humming and strumming.

Mark's looking up at the sky with the biggest smile on his face. I ask him, "Mark, what is it with the stars and moon and stuff? You're like a little kid out here."

He looks back, "That's totally it. This all reminds me of how big God is, and if He can handle all of this, He can handle all of me. It reminds me I can be free."

I nod, "That's cool. You're free, for sure, dude."

Pete is poking at the fire and smiling. He asks, "John, what do you think about when you look at the moon and the stars?"

"Just now you mean?"

He smiles back at me. Mark too is listening.

"Actually, I was thinking about Lonny."

Mark sits back from the fire, "What about him?"

"Hoping he's okay, hoping he's laughing like this with his homies somewhere."

"That's rad. He's the coolest kid," Pete says.

Mark motions toward Pete, "What about you, Pete? What were you thinking about?"

"I was thinking about Pastor Wes, actually."

Will comes back humming as Mark says, "There is something about him that's pretty different. Mrs. Johnson too."

Will stops humming long enough to say, "They have some weird connection don't they? Not as weird as Johnny Mathis and Ivy League, but a good weird." He laughs and starts strumming again.

Pete lays down on his sleeping bag, "I'm sure learning a lot from them."

"I think I learned as much from Lonny as I have from the Johnsons," I say.

"Got it guys," Will says excitedly. "It's 'Peaceful Easy Feeling.'" He plays a few chords and starts singing the chorus. I quickly join him. Will and I start laughing knowing what's coming next. Then we sing as loud as rock stars,

And I want to sleep with you in the desert tonight / With a billion stars all

around.

<h1 style="text-align:center">31.</h1>

We sleep late and then stop to help five or six cars that had broken down on I-10. Sweet Pete over there is the biggest Good Samaritan in the whole desert. Mark and Will have grease on their hands. I smell like gas, and Pete has a smile on his face.

In the Big Surf parking lot we hear music. The chorus shouts, *"God rules. God rules!"* Will puts up his hand and stops us. We stand still in the parking lot listening. Will cringes as he listens. We all look at each other shaking our heads. Even Pete stops smiling. Mercifully the song ends.

"Oh, thank God it's over," Will says. In his last word of protest, he says, "I can't believe we are spending our free time here. This is the worst idea ever."

"Marcie will be glad to see you, Will," Pete says as we walk toward the front gate.

As we come in the turnstile Pastor Wes sees us and comes toward us, "You made it! So glad to see you guys!" He leads us toward some picnic tables.

"I saved these for you boys," Mrs. Johnson says as she sets down a huge tray of food. "I had to stave off a few of the kids from the kitchen. I'm glad you made it when you did. I don't think I could have held them off much longer." Mark says something kind to her on our behalf. I'm looking for Laney but don't see her. Beth and Vista see us and squeal as they run over to hug their guys. Will and I smile and then do our own squealing, throwing our arms around each other, loudly mocking the two greatest guys we know.

Everybody cracks up. "You two were made for each other," Mark says.

Will struts toward me, "And they were naked and without shame, baby!"

Pete almost falls over from laughing, "Too much! That visual is too much!" We all laugh together and then Pete looks past me and nods.

I turn to see Laney with a few other folks laughing at us.

Laney gently applauds as I move toward her. "Great to see you. I wasn't sure if you'd make it," I say.

"I'm glad we came. This place is great. And what a show you and Will put on for us. Can't get much better than that."

"Nope. That's about as good as it gets. How was Tucson?"

"We had a great time. We saw the new movie, *The Breakfast Club.*"

"How was it?"

"It was good. A little over the top, but the message is timely."

"William, John, you guys are going to love this band," Pastor Wes says. "They're from Southern Cal, maybe you know them, John? They're called Stryper. They're really great, and they love the Lord!"

I've not seen Pastor Wes this excited all summer. We all follow his enthusiasm.

The music starts with a guitar solo that literally rivals Eddie Van Halen's *Eruption*. No lie. Will can hardly move. His mouth is gaping as this guitar player kills it. The rest of the band joins in, and they absolutely blow our minds.

The music is unbelievable. I've never heard a Christian band sound like this. The band looks like they've just come off the Sunset Strip. I can't tell if they're girls or guys. They're wearing more spandex than Mötley Crüe. We all look at each other in disbelief. After the first song Pastor Wes is bouncing around. "These guys are awesome, aren't they? Did you hear that guitar riff? And they all love the Lord!"

I try a couple of times during the first few songs to talk with Laney, but it's no use. It's too loud. In between songs, Pastor Wes is running around slapping people on the back. "Isn't this awesome? And they love the Lord!"

By the end of their set, I decide I'm a fan of Stryper, but have gotten nowhere with Laney. Right before the band leaves the stage they throw out a stack of New Testament Bibles with their *Stryper* sticker on the front. I catch one and quickly offer it to Laney. "You keep it," she says. "It will remind you of 'an awesome band who loves the Lord.'"

"How about you to keep it? It will remind you of our first concert."

"First?" she says shyly, "Will there be another one?"

"I'd like there to be. Would you be up for going sometime?"

"Sure. I'd like that."

This might actually be happening. Oh, my freaking God. I'm almost as excited as Pastor Wes. Almost.

Pastor Wes motions for us all to join him. "Thanks so much, each of you, for coming. I hope you enjoyed yourselves. I would like to ask you to pray for these musicians and their ministry. They are reaching a lot of people the Church hasn't been able to reach for a long time."

He has us circle up and hold hands right there in front of everybody. He kicks off his flip flops. I grab Laney's hand. For the first time all summer, I wish the prayer wouldn't end.

Andee is ready to go as soon as the "Amen" is pronounced: "Let's go. Van leaves in five minutes."

"Can I walk you back to the van, Laney?" I ask.

"Oh, you don't have to do that. Stay here with your friends."

Pastor Wes interrupts. "John, what did you think about the band? Weren't they the best? Had you heard of them back home?"

"No, but they were pretty rad."

Pastor Wes is not slowing down. "A few of the guys are going to go meet the band backstage. I'd love for you to come with us." He looks past me as the guys head toward the stage, "Come on, let's hurry."

I struggle to find a way out. Pastor Wes grabs my arm and pulls me out, "Come on, let's go."

"Looks like I gotta go," I say as he pulls me away. "It was really great to be with you."

"See you soon…Thanks for saving me a seat."

Pastor Wes jogs up to the rest of the crew. "This is so great. This is so great!"

PART TWO - LANEY

"What a great day," Eileen says cheerfully as we climb onto the first bench seat in the camp van.

Bernice groans as she settles into the passenger seat, "It was too long, too hot, and too loud."

Andee winces with her in mutual misery as she pulls herself behind the wheel. Adjusting the rearview mirror she says, "It was long Bernice. Way too long. But I get it. I understand what those musicians are trying to do, but they are going about it all the wrong way. Not one word from that stage about sin. Not one word of truth. She points to her Bible on the front console, "It says right here, 'If you are not for me you are against me.'"

Another wordless moan from Bernice.

Andee glances at us in the mirror and says, "Didn't hear much of any of that today, did any of you? Eileen? Laney? Thoughts?"

Eileen and I exchange quick glances. Eileen looks nervously at Andee and says, "I didn't hear much of that. I guess you're right."

"I heard it, y'all." I point to Andee's Bible, "I didn't hear it in black and white, but I heard the spirit of it in their songs, in their smiles, in their hearts. You're right, Andee. It wasn't black and white. It was full color. It was beautiful."

"Beautiful?" Andee snaps back. "Men wearing make up? Girls hardly dressed? There isn't anything good or beautiful about that!"

The van becomes oppressively quiet, marked by Eileen's sigh. I look out the window summoning courage.

Bernice turns toward Andee and in full agreement says, "And what about Pastor Wes? He totally loved it. What does that say about him?"

I answer quickly, "I think he's great. He's got a view of God that is so refreshing. When he's talking to the kids, I feel like he's talking to me."

Eileen smiles again and says, "I thought the same thing the other night. I thought he was talking right to me. I'm learning a lot."

Not surprisingly, Andee dismisses us both, "Well, you know what I think about that, Bernice. I'm putting up with him until he gets transferred out of here. He'll be gone in a summer or two just like everybody else. But, I'll still be here. This is my calling. This is my camp. No matter what so-called pastor Dr. Ron and headquarters appoints to serve here. No one knows what these campers need like I do. No one."

33.

"This is the day the Lord has made, let's rejoice and be glad in it," Pastor Wes says over the loudspeaker startling me awake. "Staff meeting will begin in thirty minutes. Looking forward to seeing everyone there."

I look over at the clock. It's 9:03. I can't believe I've slept this late. I look again at my night stand and see the Bible with the Stryper band sticker sitting on top of *Crime and Punishment*. I exhale.

As I'm washing my face there's a knock on the door, "Laney, it's Phoebe."

"Come in, girl. I'm finishing getting ready."

She sits on the foot of my bed as I pull my Ole Miss cap over my unwashed hair, "Hey, how was the break? Did you enjoy last night?" she asks.

"The break was good. Last night was so great. How about you guys?"

"I spent most of the day with Marcie. The concert last night was so awesome. I loved every minute of it."

"Me too. I've never seen anything like it." I slip on flip flops and grab my sunglasses as we head out into the morning sun.

Beth comes out of the cabin ahead of us. "Hey girls," she yells. "I was looking for you. I've got an idea."

"What are you thinking, Beth?" Phoebe asks.

"How about we get up early and walk in the mornings? I know I need the exercise. This camp food is killing me," she says as she pats her rock-hard stomach.

"For sure," Phoebe says, "What do you think, Laney?"

"Yep. I'd love that."

"I thought you guys would be up for it," Beth says, accompanied by a hand-clap. She smiles big and bright and says, "I don't have a big exercise goal or anything. I just want to do something fun—and healthy of course."

"Did you ask Marcie yet?" Phoebe says.

"I didn't ask her. I guess I should."

"I think she'd appreciate it," Phoebe says.

Beth sighs.

I slip on my sunglasses.

Beth looks over as we walk and says, "Guess I'm stealing the idea from the boys' counselors."

"How's that?" I ask.

"The boys get together and hang out at the picnic table every night after curfew. Pete says it's his favorite time of the day."

"I'm sure time with you is his favorite part of the day," I say.

"I don't think so," she says. "Those guys are pretty tight."

"I've noticed that."

"Honestly, I'm not sure if I've met boys like those boys. They're so different and yet so connected," Phoebe says as she pushes up her sunglasses.

Andee stands in the doorway, checking off names. As we approach, her demeanor changes, "Laney, may I have a minute?" She quickly turns to Beth. "Do you mind taking my place for a moment? I need to chat with Laney."

Beth reaches for the clipboard and pen, "Happy to help."

Andee slips her arm through mine and like a parental escort walks me toward the basketball court "Let's sit over here. I don't want to be interrupted."

I pull off my sunglasses so I can look her in the eyes as we sit on the bench. I assume we are going to pick up the conversation from last night.

"Laney, I was going to mention this to you last night, but to save you from embarrassment, I waited until I could speak to you privately. I want you to know that I think the world of you, and because I care, I want to suggest you keep your distance from John."

I'm taken aback but don't say anything. It's obvious she has more to say.

"I've noticed you talking with John a few times and saw the way you were carrying on during the Moonlight Hike. And then, last night at the concert. Please know I'm only speaking out of your best interest."

"Thank you. I appreciate you having my best interest in mind, but I'm good."

She interjects, "Of course you are, but it helps to have people in your life who can see your blind spots. John is in your blind spot."

"…In my blind spot?"

She leans in toward me, resting her forearms on her legs, "Let me speak truth as clearly as possible. John has a lot of baggage, Laney. He's from a very broken family. He's great with campers, I'll give him that, but it's no secret he's one slip-up from being fired. My experience tells me he won't make it through the summer and he'll leave you with a broken heart, just like every other girl who gets taken in by him."

"Thank you for your concern. I do want you to know I can handle myself, even in my blind spots. Andee, respectfully, I am a little embarrassed, but not for me or for John. For you."

"Excuse me? How so?"

"I'm uneasy you would talk like this about John, about anybody really."

She touches my leg, "Let me assure you. I've been at this a long time. I've given my life to this. I know what I'm talking about, and you are very new to it."

"That's true. I am new to this camp and these people, but I'm not new to heartbreak or messy families. That's partly why we're here, right? To learn and grow?"

She looks past me. I'm not sure she even heard what I just said.

"I'm going to have to cut this conversation short. I see some things I need to attend to immediately." She taps me on my knee again and says, "Know you've been warned."

34.

We are late getting to the campfire. My girls are tired as the last few days have been so full. The only seats left are the very top. I look for John as we get settled but don't see him.

The music from "Rapper's Delight" comes over the campfire speaker. All the kids immediately jump to their feet and start dancing. John, Pete, and Mark come from the side, each wearing black sunglasses and Hawaiian shirts. The kids cheer even louder as the boys dance across the stage.

Will quickly comes from the other side with his sunglasses and denim jacket, rapping the opening words to the song. All of my girls dance and sing wildly with him. Every girl knows every word. The four boys spread out across the front, singing and dancing, each singing a few lines of the song. They're playful and animated as they interact with each other and the rest of us. John seems so free as he claps and cheers and bounces up and down. He leans over and sings with Will, "Then you throw your hands high in the air…" Hands are up everywhere, waving back and forth. I see Pastor Wes and Mrs. Johnson breaking it down. This is the absolute best!

The party carries on for a few more verses with the kids hardly taking a breath. The song ends with the boys high fiving each other and some of the kids on the front row. Mrs. Johnson hugs Will, and he slides his sunglasses on her. She poses, lifting the sunglasses as Will runs to the side of the stage to the loudest cheers of the summer.

Somehow Pastor Wes manages to calm us all down and take us back into the Zacchaeus story he's been telling every night. He reads the story from his Bible and then closes it and smiles, "So Jesus was going on a Moonlight Hike singing 'Rapper's Delight.'" The whole camp laughs and cheers.

"And on the Moonlight Hike Jesus comes to this tree and there is this guy hanging in it. Short guy, like in the song, *Not as tall as the rest of the gang.* A guy who didn't have a date for the Hike. A guy who couldn't get a date for the Hike because nobody liked him. He couldn't even find a guy friend to walk with him.

"It was a sycamore tree, like that one back there, behind Mark's cabin. See it? Zacchaeus climbed it so he could get a better look at Jesus…Or maybe he didn't want people to see him?"

Pastor Wes starts walking toward the tree in the back of the campfire pit. He's ducking his head, then straining to see as he looks up. He points, "Man, when Jesus stopped at the bottom of this tree and chose Zacchaeus to come down and eat with Him, I was so mad! That guy? You're going to eat with that guy? Are you kidding me? That guy!"

He sits down in on the last row of campers. Everybody is staring at him as he shakes his head, "That guy, can you believe it?" He taps the kid next to him on the shoulder. "Does Jesus have a clue as to what kind of guy Zacchaeus is? He's a crook! He's a thief!"

Pastor Wes uses every bit of himself to draw us all in. Every eye and most hearts are totally focused on what he is saying, "You chose him? Of all people! He's stolen from me, my mom, and my mom's mom! Come on Jesus!"

The more he talks the more I resonate with him. I know he's talking to these kids, but I know he's talking to me too. Right to me.

He slowly stands. He stands and stares. The silence bellows into the air. It enfolds all of us. He waits. Then he softens his posture and confidently asks, "How many of you know what it feels like to be chosen like Zacchaeus? Like, out of all these churchy people, Jesus chooses an unchurchy guy? Do any of you know what it feels like to be chosen? To be sought out? Singled out? Not for something bad, no, no, but how many of you have felt chosen for something good?"

Everyone nervously looks around. A few hands go up, with Mrs. Johnson and some others down front leading the way. I look over at my girls. Not one is hand up.

Pastor Wes keeps talking to the campers right next to him. "I know what's it's like," he says. "I know what it feels like to do everything right and still not be chosen. I know how that feels, how it hurts." He looks down at the kid sitting in front of him. "It hurts bad, man. Really bad."

He looks around, making eye contact with everyone he can. His eyes just catch mine. I nod at him, surprising myself. He smiles at me, as if acknowledging my whole story, and then goes right back into the story he's telling.

"I'm standing there, right in front of Him, and Jesus chooses him! He chooses Zacchaeus! Jesus invites himself to go to Zach's house for lunch. Are you kidding me? You've got to be kidding me!"

He starts walking down the campfire pit stepping in between kids as he comes back to the front.

"Chosen," Pastor Wes says adamantly. "Chosen?" He quiets himself again and slips his hands in his pockets. He shrugs his shoulders, "I don't know what it feels like to be chosen. I know what it's like to be unchosen." I can't take my eyes off of him. My heart won't let me. *Unchosen?*

Pastor Wes raises his hand and makes an imaginary line down the amphitheater. He says, "If tonight you feel 'chosen,' I want you to move to this side of the campfire pit." He waves the other way, "But if you feel 'unchosen' I want you to get up and move to the other side." At once kids start moving around, almost all of them make their way to the unchosen side. I find myself momentarily paralyzed by the question and my answer.

"Freeze!" Pastor Wes yells. "Freeze!" The entire camp freezes. He motions for us to go back to our seats and slowly kids move back.

"You know what?" he says as everyone begins to sit back down. He puts his hand over his chest. "I am chosen. I am chosen. Just like Zacchaeus, I'm chosen and so are you. You are chosen by the Most High God and He wants you to know it. Listen family, before Jesus asks 'Zach the Unchosen' to do anything or to change or to not be a loser or a cheater, Jesus calls Zacchaeus to Himself." Pastor Wes walks slowly across the front of the stage, and says, "Jesus tells Zacchaeus, 'Come be with me. I just want you to be with me. I want to eat with you. I want to talk with you. I want to share my life with you. Would you come down and just be with me?'"

"What an invitation," I whisper toward Anna.

I look over at her and she says, "I'm unchosen." She buries her head in her hands. She's trying to be quiet and hide her tears, but it's obvious she's crying. Her pain is everywhere. I put my arm around her and pull her in. A few other girls start to cry, and before I know it, girls are crying everywhere. I have tears in my eyes, not only because of what Pastor Wes said, but because of the raw emotion coming out of these girls. I kneel down in front of them trying to pull them into a circle with me so I can hold them.

Pastor Wes ends his devotional by saying, "Jesus doesn't promise Zacchaeus that he'll get a date on the Moonlight Hike. He doesn't promise him that he'll be liked, or have a lot of friends, or become the president of his class, or make varsity, or even be popular. He just calls Zacchaeus to Himself. And that's enough. He's chosen. You are too."

Mrs. Johnson gets up, wipes her own eyes, and closes the campfire with a prayer. She prays that God would remind us all that we are "chosen." Then she dismisses us back to our cabins.

My mind is racing as to what to say to these girls. How do I follow up with that story, with their story, with mine? I want to grab John and talk with him, but before I can, Mrs. Johnson comes over and hugs Anna. All of the girls stop as Mrs. Johnson then hugs each one.

"Laney. Do you have a sec?" She looks at my girls. "I want to love on your counselor for a minute. You girls head up to your cabin."

John smiles and waves as he and his guys begin walking up the road. I wave back. Mrs. Johnson looks over her shoulder to see what's going on. She snaps back to me with a big grin. "John's quite the rapper, quite the counselor."

"He continues to surprise me."

"And me! That was the most fun I've had in a long time. Laney, I wanted to ask you about you and your girls. Tonight was pretty emotional for all of us, including me."

I look at her, not certain what I can share. "It was emotional for me too. I love what Pastor Wes said. I felt like he was talking right to me."

"You are chosen Laney. Do you believe that truth?"

"To be honest, I find it a lot easier to believe it for my girls than believing it for myself."

"I think that's a struggle for a lot of us. I can believe it for you all day long; believing it for me is not always so easy."

I look toward my girls.

She looks at them too and then back at me, "Is there a reason why you've been struggling in really believing this for yourself?"

I pause. I know if I start talking now I may not be able to stop myself.

She sees my hesitation, I hate she does, "Laney, I don't mean to push you. I'm sorry. Just know if there's anything I can do, or any way I can join you, you let me know. Okay?"

"For sure. Thanks so much for leading and loving the way you do."

35.

John and I have our campers outside the dining room as we gather for breakfast. We've been trying to find time to see each other, even if it's only for a few minutes. We sneak inside to talk while I pour a cup of coffee. He makes tea.

"Hey, Laney. How are you?"

"I'm good, John. I'm really good."

"I've seen a lot of smiles and some tears too over the last few days. I've hated not being able to really talk with you about all that was going on."

"It's been hard but really good. Last night's devotional time in the cabin was intense. I think we had a real breakthrough."

Bernice and Eileen come in to get coffee. The cook waves to Bernice, "Please tell Andee breakfast is going to be fifteen minutes late."

"Hey, looks like we might have a few minutes," I say.

We walk over toward the front window to keep an eye on our campers. "Tell me about last night," John says.

"Well, this whole 'chosen' thing, it's got my girls all wrapped up. There's so much emotion swirling in us, in me."

His eyes are comforting, "Tell me about that? I mean, if you want to."

"I want to. I do. I'm just not sure where to start. There's so much. You know?"

"I do know. This whole thing has been big with my guys." He looks out the window. "It's big in me too."

"Tell me about that? I mean if you want to," I say with a grin.

His face grows more serious, "You know the whole 'story' thing Pastor Wes keeps talks about? Mine is a mess. It's got a lot of 'unchosen' chapters in it." He pauses. He looks like he wants to say something else, but doesn't.

"Mine too," I say.

"What about that?"

I laugh nervously, "Yes, what about that?"

He looks out the window. I follow his eyes as he smiles at his campers. No one seems to notice we are still inside. He looks back at me.

"So seeing we are talking about our stories, tell me about yours, Laney. Tell me about your family. What's the best thing about your family, and what's hard about being in your family?"

"That's not a loaded question at all."

"Give it a go. I'm interested."

"Sure. My family loves me. What more do you want to know?"

"Come on, Laney. I want to know."

"Okay, I have two sisters who are much older than me, so in some respects it's like I have three moms. My dad is my hero. He smokes too much, he chews too much, but he's so good to me and my sisters and my mom. He loves my mom with everything he's got, and my mom cherishes him, for sure."

"That's so cool," he says. "Honestly, I don't think I've ever met a girl who said her dad is her hero. I want to be that dad one day."

"I'm sure you will be."

"Hope so. What's your favorite thing about your dad?"

"Oh, gosh, John. That's another deep one. When I was younger, my dad and I used to go to our little church together on Sunday nights. We'd all go in the morning, but just my dad and I would go on Sunday nights. We'd have this altar time and my dad and I would go forward every time. It was so special to me. No matter how I was doing at school or at work or whatever, he'd softly pray over me and tell God how grateful he was for allowing him to be my dad."

"No way. That's so awesome."

"It really is. And you want to know the best part?"

"Yes, tell me."

"The best part is he and I would go out for pie afterward and just sit and talk about life. It was really sweet."

"Sounds rad. Sounds like you've got a pretty great life back home."

"Yes, I do. I'm super thankful. I've got some bumps and bruises along the way. I have the scars to prove it. We don't need to get into all of that now. What about you?"

"No, no, no. Let's talk about that. I'd love to hear about that too."

His genuine interest is pulling me in. I can tell he's not trying to get any- where or score. He's not just going through the motions. I know what that feels like. This is different. I look out the window again to make sure my girls are good. Phoebe has them all circled up talking. I look back at John and decide to go ahead and risk a little more. "What's hard…what's hard is disappointing my parents. What's hard is hearing them weep over me when I come home after having too much to drink. What's hard is telling my dad I got kicked out of Ole Miss because I partied too much. What's really hard is living with all of that."

"Whoa…that is hard. It's brutal." He looks out the window, but not as his kids. He looks like he goes somewhere in his mind, just for a moment, and then comes back to me. "I'm sorry it's hard. I hate that. I know a little of that sting. It still hurts?"

"When I think about it, yes, it really hurts. I try not to think about it… talking about it with you helps."

"Talking about all of this helps me too. Laney, if you can figure out how not to think about it, will you let me know?"

"You'll be the first."

He asks about my sisters and about how I ended up at Ole Miss. He never takes his eyes off me. I want to say he loves, but that's getting way ahead of myself. Although, that's what this feels like. This feels like being chosen.

36.

"Laney," Anna says. "I think I need to go to the nurse."

"Okay, love. You're not feeling well?"

"Just stomach stuff."

"Give me a minute to grab Phoebe and ask her to keep an eye on our girls."

As we walk into the makeshift nurse's unit I'm surprised to see John sitting there. "Hey you," I say.

He springs to his feet and greets me with the best hug and warm hello.

My heart flutters. "What are you doing here? Is everything okay?"

"One of my guys has been throwing up so I brought him over." He looks at Anna, "Hey, you okay?"

She nods shyly at him and looks at me and smiles.

The nurse hears us and comes out to ask how she can help. She takes Anna into the next room.

"Saved you a seat," John says pointing to the chair. He turns in his seat looking right into me, "How are you, Laney? The last couple of days have been pretty crazy."

As I start to answer, John's camper walks out of the back room and stands in front of us. John reaches out and grabs his arm, "You feeling better, dude? Tomorrow night is the Moonlight Hike."

"A little. The nurse says she wants me to go back to the cabin and lay down for thirty minutes."

"Thirty minutes, huh?"

"Can we go?"

"Sure, give me thirty seconds. Wait outside so you can get some fresh air. I'll be thirty seconds."

"Thirty seconds," the camper says as he laughs at John.

John looks at me, "I'm so sorry. There is no other place on the planet I'd rather be than right here with you having this conversation. But this kid…"

I interrupt, "I know. And I'm thankful. Really thankful."

As he reaches for the door it opens up the other way. John almost falls forward. My heart sinks as Andee walks in.

"Another secret rendezvous, this time in the nurse's office?" Andee sneers, "John, I believe I saw one of your campers outside, alone."

John looks back at me. I speak quickly hoping to calm this quickly brewing storm, "We both ended up here at the same time with sick campers. It was serendipitous."

John waves and slips out before Andee can respond.

She walks across the room and sits in the seat next to me, "Laney, we need to chat."

"Yes, I believe we do."

"Listen, Laney. All of this is getting us nowhere." She turns fully toward me and rests her hand on my arm. "I want to speak to you 'from my heart,' I think that's your vernacular, I want to talk with you about John."

I begin to respond and then choose not to.

"Laney, I told you not long ago that John is not the kind of boy you want to get close to." She squints her eyes as she says, "You don't know him like I do. I've known him since he was a kid."

"Since he was a kid?"

"Oh, I see. You did know that he grew up out here, right? Yeah his parents were the camp pastors…that is until his mom had an affair with another pastor who just happened to be her boss, and John was the one who found them together. And then there's all the other affairs she's had. But you know about all of this, I'm sure."

"I didn't know that, I…"

She interrupts, "Ah, I knew I should have told you all of this a long time ago. It would have saved a lot of pain and hopefully kept our focus on saving children, which is why we are here." I look away as Andee leans in toward me, "Just think about all the families that family has torn apart."

I look back at her and say, "I can't imagine all the hurt."

"Yes," she says. "But at least John's mom came back to the first one. At least I think they are still living together, not married of course. You would know though, right? You and John are so close."

I adjust my sunglasses on my head, choosing my words carefully. "Yes, John and I are learning each other's stories. We are really trying hard to honor each other's stories just like Pastor Wes has asked us."

"I see. So basically, he hasn't told you anything, he's just like his mother. Keeping secrets."

"Andee, I truly believe that you believe telling me all of this is the right thing to do. But I have to tell you, this isn't right. This is John's story. It's his story to tell."

"'It's his story to tell…It's his story to tell.' I see." She throws a dart at me with her eyes. "What does John really know about your story? Have you told him your story, your whole story? Or are you still keeping secrets?"

I'm frozen, except for my heart beginning to shatter in a million pieces.

"Let's cut the Bible belt southern belle persona, Laney." She moves in with a fatal blow, "No one comes all the way across the country to work at a camp unless they are running from something. We both know why you are really here."

Anna comes out of the office, "I'm ready, Laney."

I can't move.

Anna nudges my shoulder, "Laney, I'm ready."

I turn toward Andee but she speaks first, "Thanks for the chat, Laney. Definitely serendipitous."

37.

Oh, no. How does she know? What does she know? It doesn't matter. She knows.

38.

"This rain hasn't let up all day. We are going to change our plans for the evening. No Moonlight Hike," Andee says. "Not to worry. We can do dinner and a movie in the chapel. I can bring one of my all-time favorite movies for us to watch."

I do my best to acknowledge her and to listen, but I still haven't been able to think straight since our conversation the other day. Before coming here I was sure I had convinced myself that I'd found resolve with all of it. Obviously, I'm a long way from resolve.

"Great," Beth says, "We are up for anything."

Anna overhears the change in plans, "Laney, can we go back to the cabin and get ready for tonight?"

"Sure, we'll only have a few minutes though so we'll need to be quick."

The smell of popcorn invites us into the chapel. We step over blankets and find a place near the front. John and his guys come in not too long after us. He comes straight over to me.

"Hey you," he says.

"Hey you."

A few of his boys nervously sit next to my girls. John gives the rest of the boys some direction and then turns to me, "So good to see you. How are you? How was your day?"

"It was actually really good. We've had fun. We played games, and a few of the girls even shared their stories. It was great."

A couple of John's guys are getting loud and he looks over at them. When he turns back he looks at me with a hope filled smile.

"I wanted to ask you if you had plans for the break. The guys and I are heading to Tucson. One of Will's friends is playing with his band at a little club. Pete and Mark are going to come, and I'm sure they'll invite Beth and Phoebe. Marcie will be there too for sure. Would you want to come?"

"Sure, another concert. That sounds great. Are you sure it's okay with everybody else?"

He grins, "I already told them you were coming."

"Well, I don't want to let you down. What else have you told them?"

He smiles. "I can't give all my secrets away."

"Ah, secrets…you've got them too?" I say while trying to laugh it off.

Andee sees us together and grabs the microphone, "Girl campers will sit on the right side of the chapel and the boys' cabins and boys' staff will sit on the left." Groans feel the air. John and I both shake our heads, and begin to talk our kids down from a complete overthrow of camp leadership.

As John and the boys are moving across the chapel I notice Pastor Wes hurrying through the front door. He pulls off this hood and wipes his glasses as he speaks to Will. He anxiously waves at the guy counselors, calling them over to him. He is obviously concerned.

The boys listen to him as he speaks. He points to his watch, flips up his hood on his rain jacket, and jogs out the back door.

John huddles up his boys, while I busy myself with my girls, trying not to stare.

Andee welcomes everyone to "Dinner and a Movie." Boxes of pizza arrive at the front door. "Counselors come and get pizza for your cabins."

I meet John at the pizza table. "This is crazy," he says. "There are some campers from the Wheel that haven't made it back from a morning hike. The camp director is worried. With all this rain, and the creek at flood stage, they could be in real trouble. Pastor Wes asked us to go with him to see if we can find them."

"Oh, my goodness. That's terrible. I'm glad you're going, but be careful."

"It's cool. We'll be fine." He puts his hands on my shoulders, "I'm really excited about tomorrow."

As we hug I whisper, "I'm excited too."

<h1 style="text-align:center">39.</h1>

The movie ends horrifically with a little girl being executed by a guillotine because she refuses the "mark of the beast." I'm appalled. To show a movie like this to a bunch of kids—my kids—is unbelievable!

Every girl in my cabin is in tears. In fact, just about every kid in camp is in tears. They are filled with fear about being "left behind."

Andee stands in front of us, somewhat triumphantly, as she says, "If you want to be saved from eternal punishment or from being left behind, come forward to the altar and ask Jesus into your heart."

Kids and staff alike start flooding the altar. I'm trying to catch my breath and figure out what to do. Most of my girls have gotten up and gone to the front, huddling at the corner of the altar. Anna is still sitting next to me. She's shaking and sobbing. "Anna, I need you to look at me. You are okay. I need you to help me get the girls together. We need to leave. We need to get back to the cabin."

"Okay," she says as she wipes tears from her face. I grab her and hug her, "Our God loves you, Anna. He loves you. His Story is not like what we just saw."

"Okay," she says again. "Okay."

I quickly go and tap my girls on the shoulders to come with me. Eileen moves toward some younger kids, trying to soothe their broken hearts. Mrs. Johnson reaches over to comfort some of the kitchen staff. She catches my eye as I shake my head in disbelief. She responds similarly and for a moment, I'm comforted. "I'm taking my girls back to the cabin where I can talk with them."

"That's wise, Laney. Thank you."

The girls and I run to the cabin as the rain tries to hold us back. We finally make it inside where it's warm and dry and safe. Yes, safe. I'm undone at what has happened, and I work to mend the hearts of my girls who have just been scared into heaven.

"Girls, that was not okay. What we just saw and what just happened was not okay. I'm sorry we watched that movie. I want you to know that's not the God of love that we have been talking about." My girls are totally confused. They don't know what to do or think. We talk for the next hour or so.

We finally turn a corner as Anna shakes her head and says, "That was totally ugly. What was the point?"

"I'll be honest, Anna. I'm not sure there was a point."

"It was so sad, that little girl dying and everything."

"It was sad—and not just sad, but wrong. We don't have to be afraid of God. He is for you. He's not against you."

Anna softens, "The whole thing was so stupid."

"Totally stupid," I say. The girls all laugh, and I laugh with them. Fear hasn't won.

Since it's the last night of camp we exchange addresses and the girls give clothes back that they've borrowed from one another and me. I stay up with them trying to make sure everyone is okay. I'm not okay, but I want to make sure they are.

40.

Beth startles me awake as she comes in the door, "Hey, let's go. We've got so much to celebrate." She's more spirited this morning than usual.

I still don't know exactly how to read her, but I'm pretty sure I don't like what she's thinking. I pull up and lean on my arms, "What's that, Beth?"

"What do you mean, Laney? Last night. Every single girl in my cabin made a commitment to follow Christ. I saw your whole cabin at the altar too. All of the boys' campers, John's cabin for sure, were down there. How excellent is that?"

I assumed this would be her response. "The last couple of days have been hard for me. Last night was really hard, Beth. And, it was hard for some of my girls. I'm not going to walk this morning. I'm going to spend time with my girls before they head home."

"Hard? Last night was so awesome! How could any of it have been hard? Well, on second thought, giving up sin can be hard. I get it."

"That's not what I meant."

Anna walks in holding her notebook, "Laney, can you write your phone number again?"

"Of course, love. Give it here."

Beth opens the door, "I'm going to head out," she says. "Maybe we can talk about this more on the break."

"Sure, Beth. Hey, really quick, are the boys okay?"

"I think so. I saw Will at Marcie's door late last night." She shakes her head, "So wrong." She steps outside and looks up toward the sun. Covering her eyes she yells back at me, "You sure you aren't coming? It's a spectacular day outside. All of heaven is rejoicing!"

41.

John runs in late to the staff meeting. He's quiet as he sits next to me on the floor, bumping his shoulder into mine to say hello.

Andee is basking in the afterglow of last night's perceived victories. "I'm honored to share that we had over 150 commitments to follow Christ this week. Most of those came last night." She smiles and receives the applause of the room. "Most of which happened without a Pastor Wes sermon."

As she continues with her report, John leans over and whispers, "What happened last night? My guys were totally freaked out."

I'm only slightly relieved at his words, "Oh, John, it was terrible."

Andee sees us whispering. It causes a ferocious fear to rise in me.

She's in total command and it's evident nothing is going to slow her charge toward heaven. "A great triumph was won last night. Let's rejoice in all that we have done for God. Use the break wisely and get some rest. We'll pick up with the next camp exactly where we left off."

I look at the Johnsons on the couch next to each other. I'm hoping one of them will say something. They don't say a word, not to us, not even to each other. They sit, hardly showing any signs of life. They look disconnected to what Andee is saying. Something is wrong. Maybe, it's me. Maybe they know too. With a desperation he can't see, I look at John.

The meeting ends and Danny immediately comes over as John pulls me up from the ground.

Danny steps in front of John, "Hey Laney! Last night was epic! Can't wait to enjoy all of this with you on the break. You're coming with us, right?"

I glance at John.

"I'm spending the time with John and his…"

He turns around and walks away before I can say anything.

Will high fives John and says, "Pastor Wes is going to let us take the camp van to Tucson so we can all ride together. Let's leave in 45 minutes. Sound good?"

John turns and gently asks, "You still up for all this?"

"I think so. I'm not exactly sure where I stand. Last night, Beth, the camp."

"I'm okay with that. Whatever is best for you is what I want. If you want to stay here I'll bail out and stay with you."

"No, don't do that. I wouldn't want you to miss time with your friends and Will's concert. I don't want to spoil that for him and for you."

"Laney, those guys love me and I love them, they've got my back. What's best for you?"

"What's best for me is to be away from here for a bit."

"Then let's do it. I'll save you a seat."

42.

Marcie pulls Will's box of tapes from the console onto her lap, "I'm the DJ on this trip." She looks over her shoulder, "Any requests?"

"We gotta start with Metallica's "Kill Them All," Will says.

Marcie glances at Will, not saying a word, and slips in "Paradise Theater" by Styx.

He shakes his head at her and then begins singing along.

John sings along too. He leans up toward Will and they laugh with each other as they sing.

After the song John says, "Tell us about the band we are going to see to-night?"

"They're much more Metallica than they're Styx."

"So devil worshippers?" Marcie says with a laugh.

"Oh, God, Marcie. They are not devil worshippers," Will says. "Get out the cassette, and read the lyrics. If you look closely, you'll see they aren't singing about anything evil. They're just being honest."

"At least they're honest. Good for them," John says.

Marcie turns all the way around her seat waving the cassette around as she talks, "I'm confused. Are you telling me that it is or it isn't a sin to listen to this? Is God okay with this or not?"

Pete shouts from the back of the van, "I used to think that way. Like God could only be found in churches, and church songs, and church people."

"I was that way too," Mark says. "I used to think God only showed up for the people who believed or behaved."

"Now what do you think?" John asks.

"I don't know what I believe exactly," he says. "What I'm starting to think is that God is in all of it. He's in the good and the bad. He's in the beauty and the ugly. He's in the light and the dark."

"Totally, Mark," Pete says. "That's so cool. It's like it's all intertwined, or intermingled, and God is in the mix of all of it."

"Like a big mosh pit," Will yells from the front.

Marcie laughs, "God is in the mosh pit? That would be a sight."

John smiles and taps on the back of Will's seat, "I'd like to believe that. That would be awesome."

Marcie ejects "Paradise Theater" and pops in "Kill Them All." Will plays air guitar on the steering wheel, and John is using the back of Will's seat for the drums.

After the song Marcie turns down the music and asks Will about the kids from Wagon Wheel.

John leans over and asks me, "How did it go this morning saying goodbye to Anna?"

"You remember how you felt when you said goodbye to Lonny?"

"Oh, man. So almost tears and everything?"

"No, there were tears and everything."

"I bet it was hard, especially after last night."

"It was the worst. I still can't wrap my head around why they would show that movie."

Marcie turns and yells toward the back of the van, "Pete, Will says you and Mark were the heroes of last night's story with those kids from the Wheel."

John laughs and looks over, "Marcie, those guys are the heroes of every story."

43.

We park under the neon sign that is only half lit.

Beth says, "Is this where we are going? Not sure this place looks safe?"

Will jumps out of the van as his friend comes around from the backdoor of the club.

We all stretch as we get out. I grab John's hand and squeeze it tight. He smiles at me, slightly calming me.

Will is excited and makes introductions, "Hey guys, this is Dave K. He's the lead guitar player of the band. He shreds." Now with his arm around Dave K., Will says, "Guys, this here is the reincarnation of Randy Rhoads."

Dave K. shakes his head, "Too high of praise, Will. Randy Rhoads is a god."

Will puts his hand on the Ozzy Osbourne patch on his denim jacket as John points and says, "Hey, how about a cover of "Crazy Train" tonight?" We nod like we know exactly what they're talking about.

"For sure, man," Dave K. says as he leads us in the door that puts us back stage. He introduces us to the other members of his band as they finish getting dressed. The smell of hair spray is potent.

Marcie smiles and nods toward Dave K, "What kind of eye shadow is that? I think I have the same color."

Dave K. laughs and grabs a tube off the makeshift vanity, "Raspberry."

The boys begin talking music and Phoebe looks toward me, "Let's go out and find a table."

The bar is filling up, and a we grab a table near some other girls who are touching up their make-up and hair. Marcie flirts with a few guys who come over.

The thought crosses my mind to talk with Marcie about all that is spinning in my head. She's the kind of girl I know I can trust. I bet she'd understand.

Beth is still unsure about the club, "This place is packed, girls. People are already drinking and smoking. Hope it's okay we are here."

"Here comes the first band!" Marcie says as John and the guys join us. The singer yells into the microphone, "The Boys are Back!" Cheers and whistles fill the club. As soon as the guitar player strums the first chord, Will yells at John, "Yes! Thin Lizzy!" Will jumps in front of John and they start singing with the band. They don't have a care in the world; they're totally loving this moment. Pete and Mark join in singing and jumping around too, and then they all sing with the band right on cue, *"And if the boys want to fight / you'd be let them!"*

Their freedom, if only for this moment, begins to set me free.

The music is really loud and really rowdy. We all try to dance together for a few songs but there's no room—not that we really care. By the time the band is finished, we are all sweating from the sheer body heat in the room. A haze of pot smoke give us the full concert experience.

As Dave K. and his band come on the stage, a full round of shots is delivered to our table. Will yells to the server, "We didn't order these."

"It's on the house," she yells back. "The band ordered it for you guys. Drink up."

I stand still. I see the boys looking at each other and then John glancing at me. He doesn't take a glass and his look tells me not to take one either. No one takes a shot.

The band strikes the loudest sound and flames shoot up from the sides of the stage, startling us. The boys immediately jump up and rush the stage.

We lose them in the sea of bodies flying around. Every once in a while, we see one of their heads pop up above all the others. I'm both excited and anxious for them.

Phoebe slips out while the rest of us girls are watching the band and looking for the boys. She comes back balancing an armful of soft drinks and two boxes of popcorn. She yells at Beth, "Slide those shot glasses over."

Beth shoots her look, almost like she's offended.

"I've got it," I say. I lean over and pick up the tray. I hand them to the girls behind us. One of the girls passes me a huge plate of nachos, "Fair trade! Thanks, y'all!"

I turn back just as Pete and Mark are pushing their way through the kids in the crowd and back to the table. I hand the nachos to them. Pete yells, "Thanks, Laney. You're the best."

The boys devour the drinks and then eat the last of the nachos.

Mark notices me looking for John, "John and Will are still in the mix!"

"Our boys are fine, Laney," Marcie yells. "This isn't their first time. It's not their first time at anything." She winks at me and then looks back at the stage. My heart sinks again, hearing her above the screams of Dave K.'s guitar.

Both boys reappear at the end of the first encore. They're soaked in sweat, and John's eye is swollen, though you can hardly tell from his smile. He's almost glowing. I reach for him, "Hey you, looks like you're bringing part of the show back to camp."

He winces as he touches his cheek, "I think God may have punched me in the mosh pit."

"He got you good if He did."

Will and Marcie start dancing and it doesn't take long before they're all over each other. John and I exchange looks while we sway along with the music. I wait on him but he doesn't move much closer. The song ends and we all cheer. Dave K. steps to the microphone, "We are going to finish with one last song, "Boom, Boom, Out Go the Lights."

I grab John, "I know this one! It's a great party song!"

"No way, that's awesome!"

All the boys circle back up and are in unison with the singer, *"No kiddin', I'm ready to fight…Boom, Boom."* And we all shout back *"Out go the lights!"* The room is at its loudest as the band sings to us, *"Boom, Boom,"* and we sing it back, *"Out go the lights!"* Dave K. plays a solo and fire shoots from the sides of the stage. The band ends with one last call back, *"Boom. Boom"* and we scream at the top of our lungs, *"Out go the lights."*

44.

The music in the van is not near as loud on the way back to camp. Marcie chose Billy Joel to accompany us. By the time we are halfway back to camp, each couple has their own conversation going.

"You were having such a good time at the concert, John."

"I loved it. It was a few hours of being free of all the responsibilities and pressures, of everything. Music has always put me on another planet…and hey, and I saw you belting it out during that last song."

"I've learned a few party songs in my day."

"Yes you have. It's awesome. Can I say, the best part of the night was that part, singing along with you."

"Thanks. It's good for me to sing with you, and to be here with you."

Will turns off the headlights.

"Boom, boom out go the lights," Marcie says as we drive slowly into camp.

It's a few minutes past curfew and we don't want to get caught. Will parks in front of the girls' cabins, and we all get out and stand together on the road. The sky seems brighter tonight than any other this summer. The stars are majestic.

Will and Marcie walk toward her cabin and go inside. Pete and Beth walk toward her cabin and stop at a bench. Mark, Phoebe, John, and I stand together as Mark points out some constellations. I glance at John while he's listening to Mark. Eventually John looks my way and says, "Let me walk you to your cabin."

We walk together, and I slip my arm through his.

"How about you and I spend the morning together, Laney? I want to take you down to this really cool spot on the creek."

"I'm up for that. It will be your turn to start talking. I feel like I've said a lot, maybe too much, and you still haven't told me much about you."

He pulls my arm out of his and holds my hand. He looks me in the eyes, "You haven't said too much, what's that about?"

I try and push it all away, "Nothing, I sometimes think I say too much, and at other times not enough."

We stand face to face. He puts his hands on my arms. Just his countenance assures me, "Come on, Laney. What are you talking about?"

"Nothing. I'm being silly."

He smiles the most strengthening smile.

"Okay. What's one thing you'd like to know about me? I'll tell you right now. Anything."

My mind of course races back to my conversation with Andee, both of them actually, but then I choose something less explosive and land on something significant from our evening. "I do have a question."

"Sure, anything."

"Do you drink?" He looks away. I've embarrassed him. I quickly reach for him. "It's okay if you do, and it's okay if you don't. No one drank at the concert even though there was a table full of shots."

His smile fades. I know he's thinking about how much he can trust me. He looks me straight in the eyes and says, "I have gotten into a lot of trouble when I drink so I try not to drink if I can manage. Every once in a while, I can't manage and I drink. Tonight, I was able to manage."

"When was the last time you couldn't manage?"

He looks away again.

I fear I may have pushed him too far. He looks back at me and barely nods and barely smiles and then stares straight into my soul as if he's searching for a place big enough to share a part of him.

He looks up, "Let's see, the last time I couldn't manage…" Now looking straight at me and without hesitation he says, "Well, it wasn't that long ago, in fact pretty recently, but there wasn't any alcohol to help me manage, so I didn't."

"What happened?"

He pulls back and laughs a little, "Laney, there's a lot of my story that I'm still learning how to manage. Right now, right here with you, I can manage."

"That's good enough for me. Thanks for sharing that with me."

"I feel like we've just had an altar time and I should take you for pie or something."

"I'd love that."

"We can sneak down to the kitchen and make some pie if you're up for it?"

"Oh, I make a mean key lime pie."

"Let's do it."

"Maybe we better wait on that one. A girl can't give away all her secrets on her first date. Breakfast in the morning will have to do." I pause, and he sees my uncertainty. "Can I ask you one more thing?"

"Sure."

"Will you tell me when you can't?"

He looks and nods, never taking his eyes of me, "When I can't what?"

"When you can't manage."

He smiles again, leans in and kisses me on the cheek. "I promise. I will if you will. Night, Laney."

45.

As we clean the table after breakfast I notice Mrs. Johnson wiping tears from her eyes. Pastor Wes slowly stands and taps the microphone. Andee rests her hand on Mrs. Johnson's shoulder as my heart starts to sink. All the fear that had been tamped down instantly surfaces.

Pastor Wes' voice cracks as he speaks, "It's come to my attention that several staff members were in violation of the camp staff covenant over the break." The room becomes deathly silent. "I've learned that alcohol has been consumed by some of our staff and that not only breaks our covenant, it breaks our bond of trust."

No one moves. Except John. He hangs his head and then very slowly shakes it.

I exhale.

"Those of you who have broken our covenant in this way or in any way over the break, please come and see me in my office. I'll be there for the next sixty minutes. Until then I'd like everyone to take on a posture of silence and solitude. I'll let you know when it's time to reconnect as a community. Please finish your breakfast in silence. You are dismissed."

Beth immediately busies herself with our plates. Pete gets up to help her. Marcie and Will start whispering. John and Mark exchange glances.

I lean into him.

He whispers to me, "Man, I hate this b.s."

The dining room slowly clears and the staff begin to disperse. Andee has followed the Johnsons toward the office. Mrs. Johnson kisses Pastor Wes and walks alone toward their cabin. Pastor Wes walks into the office with his head hung low. Andee is looking over her shoulder to see if anyone is coming.

As John and I walk he whispers, "You going to be okay?"

"I'm fine. I think. Are you okay?"

"I really, really hate this stuff. I despise it. It's rumors and innuendos. If he knew someone did something he'd go and address the person directly. This is b.s. and it crawls all over me."

"It bothers me too. Can we sneak away and talk?"

"They're watching us. I don't want to get you into any more trouble. As long as you're okay, let's catch up later."

"I'm okay."

"See you in a bit," he whispers as he turns toward the bridge.

"Can't wait."

A few people begin to line up outside of Pastor Wes' office. By the time I walk past the office to my cabin, about ten people are standing there. It's a bunch of kids on the kitchen staff. Maybe the whole kitchen staff, I can't tell. I walk by the office as quickly as I can thankful it's not me this time.

I try to busy myself with *Crime and Punishment,* not really paying attention to a single word on the page. An hour goes by before there's finally a break in the silence. Pastor Wes' voice comes over the loudspeaker. "John and William, please report to the office." My heart stops. Pastor Wes says it again. "John and William, please report to the office."

I put down the book and open my cabin door to look around. I'm not sure what I'm looking for. Phoebe's sitting on the bench outside her cabin and sees me. She waves for me to come down to her cabin. She runs over and knocks on Beth and Marcie's door. A few moments later we are huddled up in Phoebe's cabin.

"What is going on?" Beth says.

Phoebe peers out the back window, "Let's see if we can find out." From there she can see the road in front of the office.

We all look at each other. Marcie looks very worried, "Did John and Will break the covenant?"

Phoebe, still looking out the window says, "What covenant? I'm so lost right now." She looks back at us.

"Surely they are fine," Beth says. "I'm just glad it's not Pete."

Marcie shoots her a disgusted look. Beth's words don't surprise me.

"Listen, I know I'm the new girl here," I say, "But John and Will are pretty amazing boys. There's no way they did anything that wrong. I'm choosing to believe the best."

Marcie shakes her head, "You're new to all this, Laney. It's Andee's way, and if she finds even a hint of something sinful, she'll pour gasoline on it just to watch us burn."

Her words are piercing.

Beth crosses her arms and says, "Marcie, stop blaming Andee for everything."

Marcie steps toward her, "I've had it with you standing up for Andee. You've been doing it all summer. You've been doing it since we were kids!"

"She's done nothing but take care of us since we were kids."

"Us! She's done nothing but take care of you, Beth. She doesn't know me at all; she's never known me."

Phoebe interrupts, "Girls, we've had this conversation. Now is not the time to have it again."

"God, Beth!" Marcie shakes her head and turns back toward the window.

I'm so unsettled by all of this, "Did we do something wrong last night? I mean other than coming in a few minutes late from the concert?"

Beth pulls her hair back and twists it into a ponytail, "I bet it was the concert. It wasn't a Christian band. It was in a bar. We shouldn't have been there."

Marcie throws her arms in the air, "Come on, seriously? No one did anything wrong. No one had sex or got high. No one even touched a drink, did they?"

"No," I say. "I thought it was a great night. How could anyone find trouble with that?"

"Andee will," Marcie says in defeat.

Phoebe reports from the windowsill, "Still no one out there."

I'm as nervous as I can be but don't say anything.

"Wait," Phoebe turns and looks back at us and then back out the window. "Oh my God. *Those boys…*"

Marcie turns around almost knocking Beth over straining to see out the window, "What? Phoebe!"

Phoebe shakes her head still looking out the window, "Would it surprise you if I said all four of them are walking into the office together?" We all crowd around the little window. "They'll be fine…I think they'll be fine…Pastor Wes likes those guys. Mark said Pastor Wes has made a few comments about how they remind him of his years working out at camp."

"When did Pastor Wes work here?" I ask.

"He worked when John's parents were here."

"Pastor Wes worked with John's parents? Wait…"

Marcie turns toward me, "Oh, sh*t, Laney. You didn't know about all that? You know John's parents were the pastors out here when he was a kid, right?"

"I do know. I don't know the whole story, but I know that much."

Marcie looks at me with genuine sympathy, "I'm sorry, Laney. It's his story to tell. If you guys keep hanging out together I'm sure he'll tell it."

"I'm sure he will," and then mumble to myself, "I hope I will."

Marcie tries to be reassuring, "Will says John doesn't talk about it unless he really trusts you. I've actually never been told about the details. Not sure what that says about me." The other girls nod along. They've never heard anything from John either. Not that any of it's comforting.

Phoebe looks back out the window, "They all went in."

Marcie tries to convince herself and me, "They'll be fine. We'll be fine."

PART THREE - PASTOR WES

"William, when you asked to use the camp van for the break you didn't say you were going to a rock concert in a bar."

"You didn't ask, Pastor Wes."

"I shouldn't have to ask. You guys know better than to take a van with the name of our camp emblazoned across it to a bar."

Andee interrupts, "Were you drinking? Obviously, alcohol was there. Probably marijuana too. Did you get drunk *and* high?"

"Wait a minute, what is this?" Pete says, lifting both hands like he's being arrested, "Can we have a conversation here without getting crazy?"

Mark quickly adds, "I don't see how this fits with our staff covenant of 'filling the gaps with trust' and 'believing the best about each other.'"

"You two weren't asked to come to this meeting," Andee says, waving her clipboard at Mark and Pete. "We don't have a problem with either of you." She points directly at John and William. "It's these two who are the problem. They've always been the problem."

William grits his teeth, "How are we the problem this time?"

"Andee, please stick to the facts," I say.

"Fine, you want the facts? Here's a list. Any one of these violates our covenant. You choose what you'd like to use on the report to Dr. Ron at headquarters. You're the boss." She starts reading from her clipboard, "Let me start with the party last summer. The one John and Will took Jenny Brown to, your predecessor's daughter...The same Jenny Brown who was underage and ended up having to get her stomach pumped because of the amount of alcohol she consumed. The same Jenny Brown whom I believe is your goddaughter, Pastor Wes?"

My anger rises and my heart sinks as I hear her words, "Yes, she is, Andee. And I love Jenny with everything in me, and her parents."

"Well, how are they anyway, now that they have left the ministry?"

Trying to control myself I quickly say, "Andee, this is not the time or the place." I look at the boys, wanting to protect them from of all of this and realize it's way too late for that.

Mark, Pete, and William shuffle in their seats, but John sits still. He appears to be disconnected as he stares out the window, but I'm pretty sure he's listening to every single word.

"Right, you just wanted the facts," Andee says sarcastically. She points again to her clipboard. "There's the night John and Will snuck out after curfew and met some girls from Wagon Wheel in the canyon...They were in a bar where Will bought drinks for everyone and John and Will got drunk."

William can't sit still. He looks like he's about to erupt as Andee charges forward.

"They purposefully ignore policy by breaking curfew and staying out all night at the picnic table… All four have broken into the canteen and have committed theft… They arrived after curfew last night…There are others but I'll stop here."

"And these are facts, Andee? You can prove all of this?"

"Not entirely…not by the letter of the law, but certainly by the spirit of the law. I may not have witnessed any of these things, but I completely believe it in my spirit."

John looks toward the other guys and then turns and looks directly at Andee. He speaks calmly, "So God told you we did all those things?"

Andee is at her self-righteous worst, "I have the gift of discernment, John. So yes."

John looks back out the window and then back at Andee. "That's not God. That's b.s."

"How dare you, John. How dare you!" Andee slams her clipboard down, "This is an outrage. If nothing else, that blatant disrespect is enough!" She looks at me as she grabs some papers and file folders attaching them to her clipboard and says, "I know Dr. Ron appointed you as the pastor, I know he says you're the boss, but if you won't handle this, I will!" and then storms out of the office.

I've blown it. I should have never given Andee the opportunity to speak like that. I should have handled this myself. The looks on the faces of these boys are piercing. I start to grasp, trying to save all of this, "William? John? Anything else you want to say?"

William is exasperated. He's trying to calm himself as he begins to speak, all the while not looking at me. "We didn't get Jenny drunk last summer. We didn't drink last night. We do regularly break into the canteen, but Sweet Pete over there ends up paying for it all the next day." He stops and looks up at me and says, "This, right here, this isn't cool."

"No, it's not. Thank you, William." I look over at John, "John?"

He doesn't hesitate, "If this is the God you want these kids to love, He's not the God for me. And I'm pretty sure He's not the God for them." He stands to leave.

"John, that's a pretty big leap."

Mark stands quickly, interrupting before John can respond. "Pastor Wes, it's obvious to us that you think differently than a lot of Christians we know. All four of us are drawn to you. We've talked about it, but this, right here, is not at all in line with what you've been teaching about. It's not. We trust you and we'll abide by whatever decision you make. But, respectfully, whatever decision is made we are going to respond together. All together."

"I hear you. I hear all of you and I appreciate you taking a stand. Listen, I'm really frustrated and angry. Let's do this: let's end this conversation here, give ourselves some space, and then let's circle back."

Mark nods and without looking at the other guys says, "That sounds great to us. Thanks, Pastor Wes." Slowly they walk out the door.

47

"Wesley, what's going on out there? I received a very disconcerting call from Andee last night. I'm hoping by now you have a handle on everything?"

"Yes, sir. I believe I do."

"Good to hear. Tell me some good news and then we'll wade into the deep water together."

"Thanks, Dr. Ron. The good news is we have had two really great camps. Kids have been encouraged and challenged. Many have made decisions to follow Christ. Record numbers actually, which is good seeing we have two camps left. And we are currently under budget."

"That is good news. Now tell me about the underage drinking and all."

Anger mixed with disappointment begins to rise in me as my mind races. "Yes, our kitchen staff all experimented with alcohol during our last break day. It happened outside camp property. Somehow they joined a party with some local kids who were camping in the canyon. A few of our kids got drunk, some got pretty sick."

"I see. Are there any liabilities you foresee with this episode?"

"Unfortunately, yes. There are a few liabilities."

"I understand. I'll have the legal department call you and you can work through each of those issues together."

"Thank you, Dr. Ron. We'll look forward to their wise counsel."

"Wesley, tell me about the insubordination of your counselors? I understand they have little respect for authority, especially the Cunningham boy."

"No sir, that is not the case. They are actually great counselors and are generally respectful, including John Cunningham."

"I see. Andee seems to think differently."

"Dr. Ron, Andee and I see a lot of things differently."

"Can you assure me that these situations, especially this one with the Cunningham boy, will be fixed?"

"I can promise you I will do my best with each of these situations."

"Fine. That will be all."

"Dr. Ron, this is all so much, do you have another minute or two?

"I am sorry, Wesley. I don't have time right now. I'll need to make a few calls up the chain and ensure the 'higher-ups' know what's happening there."

"I understand."

"Wesley, are you sure you can pull this together, or should we send in the cavalry?"

"No need for the cavalry. Your prayers are our biggest need."

"Of course. You know you and your wife are on our list. I'll be in touch."

As I hang up the phone, the heaviness overwhelms me. I bury my face in my hands. I hear some kids laughing, sounding as if they don't have a care in the world as they walk past the office. I look up to see them, but miss them. I grab my Bible off of the corner of my desk. I flip through it looking for some words of hope or courage. I can't find any. They all look the same.

48.

I stand pretty defeated in front of the campers and staff. Every eye is on me. Every eye except the guy counselors. They haven't looked my way since our meeting the other day in the office. I can't look at Andee.

"Yay, Pastor Wes!" a kid shouts from the back. A few kids giggle with him.

"Yay for you too!" I shout back. A few more kids laugh.

The laughter lifts me a sliver. Enough to get me started. Enough to get me to go back.

"Family, I'm going to talk about something a little different than I have the past few nights. I'm actually going to talk about something I learned a long time ago, when I was sitting right where you were. I want to talk about some truths that are really important to me." A few staff members exchange glances. Sheri smiles the most reassuring smile.

"Anyone ever heard of Psalm 23?" A few kids smile, a few kids sigh, almost like, 'here we go again.' I nod toward the smiles, "The Lord is my shepherd?"

I open my Bible, flipping to Psalm 23. I look up expectantly, and see some heads turn away looking toward the road. Andee gets up and walks out of the Campfire Pit toward a couple of people who are walking slowly toward us. Sheri sees this too and gets up and walks toward our visitors. It's Dr. Ron and his wife. The life that was arising within me moments ago immediately drains.

I try not to show my embarrassment while I say, "Campers, as you can see we have a few visitors to camp tonight. Sheri, can you bring our guests forward and introduce them to everyone?" Sheri forces a smile, and then escorts the Hills up front, next to me. Andee almost strutting, as she flanks the side of Mrs. Hill.

"Campers and staff, these are some very precious people to Pastor Wes and me. Like Pastor Wes is our pastor here, and maybe you have a pastor back in your church, this is Dr. Ron, and Mrs. Hill. They are our pastors. Please give them a warm camp welcome."

The kids applaud politely, not having any idea who these people are, and most of them couldn't care less. The staff is watching too. A couple of the kitchen crew begin whispering. I glance toward the guy counselors. They are watching me. They know what's going on.

Sheri helps the Hills to find a place in the front row. Sheri sits on one side, Andee on the other. My mind goes to the time when Dr. Hill was a much younger man and he and my dad played basketball together. He was Ronny back then. He's much older now – Dr. Ron now. Sheri nods at me, encouraging me.

"As I was saying, I want us to take a journey deep into Psalm 23, and I want you to join me. Whoever you are, wherever you are, I want you to step into this very sacred story, God's story, my story, and it's your story too."

Dr. Ron crosses his arms as Mrs. Hill opens her big Bible.

"For the next couple of nights, I want to tell you about God being our Good Shepherd. I'm going to start us out tonight talking about something that means a lot to me. A whole lot. And then each night, we'll talk about another scene in the story, wrapping it all up on the Moonlight Hike."

A few kids smile at the thought of the Moonlight Hike.

"It starts this way, *'The Lord is my Shepherd, I shall not want.'*" I nod, reminding myself more than anything. I press ahead by asking the kids a question, "I think most of a know what a shepherd is, or what a shepherd does. Someone tell me what a shepherd does."

A few younger kids speak up from the back.

"That's right. They feed sheep. They care for the sheep."

A few other phrases come from the front.

"Yes, they protect the sheep." I'm starting to gather strength as I'm reminded of the power of this truth. "That's a big one. Let me ask one more question. The Bible says, *Jesus is our Good Shepherd. He lays down His life for His sheep.'* If He's the Shepherd what does that make us?"

Kids shout out from all over the campfire pit, "Sheep. Sheep." An energy starts to build.

"Oh, and do you know I just learned something about sheep. Sheep are dumb animals. They do dumb things. They are like, big time followers. My dad used to say 'sheep are the dumbest animals in all of creation.' Sheep can be stupid sometimes. Did you know that?"

Kids are laughing a little and looking at each other.

I look around and quickly rub my hands together, "So, if the Bible is saying we are like sheep, is the Bible saying we are stupid?"

Now it's a little nervous laughter.

"Yes!" I say as enthusiastically as I can muster. "Of course, you're not stupid, but we all do stupid things sometimes, don't we?" I glance at Dr. Ron; he's stoic, Mrs. Hill is smiling. Mrs. Hill always smiles.

"Anyone here every done anything stupid?" Heads nod and a few fingers point, there's a little laughter coming from the older kids. "Of course. Everyone has. I have. Our Camp Director, Andee has. And, I have to be careful here because I don't want to get in trouble, but I would bet even our special guests here tonight have done some stupid things once or twice." I laugh and take a step toward them, "but only once or twice, right Pastor Hill?" He nods in agreement. Mrs. Hill doesn't move. Her permanent smile remaining permanent.

I glance at Sheri who is fiddling with her necklace. It's what she does when she's anxious.

I keep going. "But check this out, check this out. The Bible says *'The Lord is our Shepherd I shall not be in want'*. A better way to say this is, *"The Lord is my Shepherd. I lack nothing."* I kneel down in front of a little boy on the front row, "You lack nothing." I point at a girl in the middle row, "You lack nothing." I see Dr. Ron gently nod in agreement. "If the Lord is your Shepherd, you lack nothing." I walk up into the sea of kids, kneeling before one teenage girl, "You lack nothing." The moment is quiet as Truth begins to grab hold of hearts and minds. "You lack nothing," I say over them all. "Tell the person sitting next to you, 'you lack nothing.'" It takes only a moment and kids are talking and smiling and some even laughing. I raise my hands to quiet them down to make sure they got it. "It's a hard concept to grasp, I know, but no matter what stupid thing you've done, or said, or believed, I want you to know you lack nothing. Nothing."

I step back in front of everyone looking around and seeing more smiles than I've seen all week.

"Pete, Beth, will you come lead us in a song, and then Pastor Hill after we sing will you come and say our closing prayer?"

Pete jumps up and bounds down to the front as I sit next to Sheri and grab her hand. She leans over and whispers, "You lack nothing." She rests her head on my shoulder while we sing a quiet song.

Dr. Ron gives the final prayer and dismisses everyone. I sit up, strengthening myself as he comes and sits next to me. "That was a fine talk, Wesley. You've gotten so much better."

"Thank you, Dr. Ron."

"I'd like a few words with you in the morning. Let's have breakfast together first thing. I'll need to get back to headquarters before lunch."

"Certainly. I look forward to it." I'll be relieved to get it over with.

"Wesley, one more thing. I think it would be important for Andee to join us. We can lean on her years of camp experience in how best to deal with all this." He sees my hesitation. "Go ahead, son. Speak freely."

The very core of my being begins to protest. I try not to show it. "I'm surprised you are here. You didn't call or let me know. Did Andee call you again?"

"She did. But let's not make this about her. The truth is Wesley, I was planning on coming anyway. I think this all might be too much for you, with all that you have going on." He sighs and rests his hands on his knees. "Let's get some rest and we'll have a brighter outlook tomorrow. Tomorrow is a new day."

49.

I'm not sure I slept last night. It was one of those nights where I was reminded of every stupid thing I've ever done. I've already had three cups of coffee by the time Dr. Ron shows up.

"Sit down, sit down, Wesley."

"Can I pour you a cup of coffee?"

"Yes, if it's hot."

"Dr. Ron, I suggested to Andee that she join us after breakfast. I hope that's okay."

"That's fine, Wesley. I'd like to hear your plans regarding the boy counselors, especially the Cunningham boy. His blatant disrespect toward policy and leadership is completely out of line."

"Sir, if anyone is being disrespectful toward leadership, it's Andee."

"Now, son, don't make this about Andee. You know better than that."

He sees me searching, "Why are you getting defensive, Wesley?"

"I'm not getting defensive, nor am I getting angry. I just want to be sure you understand my position, my perspective."

"I appreciate your feelings and sensitivity. But enough of that. Let's not make this about you. Now tell me about the Cunningham boy. Is he as toxic as he sounds? Has he in fact infected the rest of the staff with a spirit of negativity? You know that was so much a part of his mother's character."

"Dr. Ron, respectfully, I don't really believe it's right to characterize John that way. He's actually a great kid. He's lived so long in the shadow of his parents. He really needs someone to believe in him, that's what I am trying to do."

"At the cost of the entire staff…of this entire program?"

"No, sir. That's not remotely true. It's not like that at all."

"Wesley, can I share a little wisdom with you. Sometimes it's better for the 99 if you let the 1 go."

"You can't mean that. That's not even…"

He interrupts. "I do mean that. I know what's best."

"But if John, or any of these guys, were to leave now, I believe they would not just leave the camp, but they might leave the Church, John for sure."

"Then you aren't doing enough to help him understand the Truth."

"I'm doing the best I can."

He sits back and takes a sip of coffee. Then leans forward and says softly, "I tell you what, I'll let you finish out the summer, but I think we may need to find another place for you to do ministry at summers end."

I'm stunned, completely blindsided. "This is the best place for us."

"I am sure there are other places where you might be of service. Let's talk about it at the end of the summer. I believe that will be all for now."

"You are making this decision without knowing the full story. Andee is not telling you the whole story. We both know her at her best and when she's not."

"We do. We do know her at her best, don't we Wesley. And quite frankly, this is not your best. Please try to keep things under control. I don't want to have to come back out here. Greet your wife for me. I'll see Andee on my way out."

50.

I don't know where to begin with all of this. My leadership, our future. I don't want to end up another casualty of ministry. And then all of that crossfire that is happening here, the wounds are everywhere. My heart aches.

We were so excited to be coming back here. This is not what we had envisioned, not what I thought things would be like for sure. My time as a staff member was some of my greatest joys in life. This was such a place of healing for me. I want that so badly for these kids.

I'd give anything to go back to that time where I just worked with kids, played basketball with them, looked them in the eyes and blessed them, loved them. There's a world of difference between loving people and leading people. I don't want to lead people to some other place. I just want to love them right where they are, just as they are.

51.

After another sleepless night, I'm up early making coffee. I slip off the kitchen counter and pour Sheri a cup as she comes down the hall, "Morning, Sheri. Here you go. It's hot."

"Morning. Thanks…You didn't sleep well again last night did you, Wesley?"

"Not really. I haven't slept well the last few nights. I keep playing all this over and over in my mind. I'm sorry if I kept you awake."

She breathes in the aroma and takes a sip, "Not bad."

"Thanks…Sheri, did you know the girl counselors get up early every morning and go for a walk? I saw them the other morning when I was on my run. Totally against the rules, leaving their kids like that."

She takes another sip. "No, I didn't know that. I wish they would have invited me. I think I'll ask Laney if I can join them. Did you know the guy counselors sit out at the picnic table every night after curfew?"

"So, I've heard," I say as I hop back up on the counter.

"Wesley, why don't you go sit with them one night?"

"What do you mean, like affirm them breaking policy?"

"No. I think sitting with them might affirm them."

"So, go up there and say, 'Hey guys, I know you're out after curfew sitting around talking about us. How about I join you tonight?'"

"Sure. That would work."

"Come on, Sheri. I can't do that."

"Why not? They like you, Wesley. They even told you that the other day in 'the meeting from hell.' And the truth is, you like them. I really like them!"

I slip back off the edge of the counter, "I think I'll do it. I'll do it tonight. But, I think I'll surprise them."

She smiles and raises her cup toward me, "I bet you'll be the one surprised!"

<h1 align="center">52.</h1>

"Don't get caught out past curfew," she whispers. I slide the book out of her hands and kiss her on the forehead as she rolls over.

I slip out into the peace of the night. Camp is its most poetic when it's quiet like this, or the exact opposite – filled with the sound of kids singing and cheering and laughing. There's nothing better in the world. I walk down to the canteen to get some snacks. I haven't a clue as to what to get so I grab one of everything.

As I come up the hill I can see all the lights off in the cabins. It's serene and still. I listen but don't hear any voices. I look over toward the picnic table but don't see anyone. I keep looking until I can see clearly that no one is there. I set all the snacks down on the table.

I'm at peace for the first few minutes and then I start to get a little anxious. I pray for a few moments, but can't stay focused. I think about the few years I was a counselor sitting at this very same table, playing board games with the other guy counselors. I so miss those days of freedom. I had such hope of who I would be. This version of me is not always it.

My mind wanders back to the four boys, "What if they're out in the canyon? What if they're up in the girl's cabins? Or worse yet, what if they see me sitting out here and decide not to come?"

It's now an hour past curfew. I debate about going up and knocking on Mark's door to see if they are there. Then decide I don't really want to know.

53.

"Thank you for the call…Yes…Will do…God bless you too." I hang up the phone and glance out into the secretary's office to see a handful of kids lined up for discipline, or because they are homesick, or a combination of both.

Sheri walks in cheerfully until she sees the look on my face, "Who was that, Wesley? Please don't tell me it was Dr. Ron again."

"I actually wish it was…It was Pat Cunningham."

She gasps, covering her mouth, "Seriously? Please tell me she was calling to check on the weather?"

"Nope. She's heard. Andee must have called her too."

"Wow. Who hasn't she called?"

"Who knows. She said she wants John to come home or she'll come here."

"That kid, my heart hurts for him."

"Mine too. I hate this for him."

Sheri shakes her head and pulls her chair up to her desk so she can look directly at me. "Pat was such a hero of mine when we were growing up."

"And then it all blew up." I come around and sit at the edge of her desk and look out the window. From here you can see the basketball court and the canteen. Life runs past the window. "Wish I could help him put some of it back together."

"Has he ever said anything to you about it?"

"Not a word. To be honest John doesn't say much to me at all. There's no one around here more energetic and engaged with their campers, but with me he's distant. It's like he's waiting for me to fail."

She grins at me and says, "He'll come around…and when you do fail, make sure he sees grace. I bet he's never seen it before."

"You're right. Grace. He doesn't just need grace. He needs to know grace upon grace. That's what I want for him. That's what I want for all of us. For you and me too."

"So what does it look like today with Pat, with John?"

"It starts with me and you right here, right now, and then with me and John. I need to talk with him. Can you check the schedule and see where he is? I don't want to call him down here. I'll go to him."

Sheri's desk is immaculate. She points to the daily schedule, "Says here his cabin should be at the pool."

"Great. I'll go up there now."

"Grace upon grace, Wes."

<h1 style="text-align:center">54.</h1>

I hear John's cheerleading above the splashing as I walk through the gate. I stop to say hello to Danny, "Hey, lifeguard. How are things up there?"

He straightens up in his chair, "Hey, Pastor Wes."

A few kids say hello to me from the side of the pool, and I yell back, "Hey guys!"

One girl, who is holding on to the edge of the pool, says, "Pastor Wes, I like what you said about the sheep. You lack nothing."

I kneel down in front of her, "Neither do you. God thinks the world of you. You know that?"

She giggles and submerges herself into the water.

A few other kids come over as I sit on the bench and watch the kids play. I don't know why I let my work keep me in my office so much when the real work is out here with kids.

When Danny sees me sitting on the bench he springs out of his lifeguard chair and is on the deck as if he's ready to rescue a swimmer. "Everything okay, Pastor Wes? You need me for something?"

"Everything is fine, Danny. The pool looks great. Guess those new chemicals we ordered are working well? The pool should be pristine with the cost of those things."

"Yes, sir. They're working great. Um, you sure you don't need anything?"

"No, I'm going to hang out with John for a moment."

"Oh, I'll get him for you. He's playing water polo with his cabin."

"No need. No need. I'll wait until the game is over."

Danny spins around, "I'll get him." Before I can stop him, Danny blows his whistle. Everyone freezes and turns toward him. He yells, "John, Pastor Wes needs to talk to you." He blows the whistle again and motions for everyone to go back to playing. I see John look over. He grabs the side of the pool and submerges.

He crawls out of the pool and pulls his towel off the fence. He walks slowly, beginning to stand upright as he comes toward me. Anxiety floods his already anxious face, "You need to see me?"

"Sit down, John. I want to talk for a second."

He wipes his arms with his towel and sits down.

"Your mom called."

Anguish replaces his anxiety, "What about my mom?"

"Everything is fine. She called to check on you."

"I bet she did. What's going on Pastor Wes?"

"Somehow she heard about our meeting and some of the accusations and she is concerned."

"She heard about all of that? You called her?"

"No. She called me."

"Who called her? Did Dr. Hill call her? Never mind."

"I don't know how she found out, or..."

He interrupts, "It was Andee. I bet it was her. God."

"John. I don't know how she knows. She says she wants you to call her and make plans to come home on the break or she'll come out here to see you."

His face changes from anguish to disgust, "She's going to do whatever she wants. She always does."

We sit in the tension for a moment. "Do you want to talk about it?" I ask.

"Talk about what, Pastor Wes? Talk about what? Is there anything else?"

I tap him on the leg, "Hold on. It's okay. I'm for you. I'm for you, John."

"Fine. What do you want to talk about?"

"I don't know…how you're dealing with all of this, your parents, your brother?"

He wipes his face again, "I don't really have anything to say about any of that."

"Okay, well if you change your mind and want to talk let me know, okay?"

He tries to smile then looks away toward his campers. He looks back at me as he gets up. "For sure. Sounds good." Danny turns back around in his chair. I hadn't noticed but Danny was watching this whole thing.

"Hey, John," I say. "Don't wear yourself out in the pool. We are going to need all of your energy in the big game tomorrow night against Wagon Wheel."

"Don't worry," he says loudly as he walks away. "I'll have enough energy to get the ball to Will. That's our whole strategy."

55.

"C-A-N-Y-O-N!" Our campers are cheering loudly and wildly waving signs and posters, chanting together as the bus from Wagon Wheel opens its doors. They too come with signs and songs. It's a festive evening. Everyone is excited.

William, John, and the rest of the team are warming up on the far side of the court. Sheri and I walk up to half court meeting Mike, the Camp Director from Wagon Wheel, "Hey, Mike. It's great to have you on our turf this summer."

"Evening Sheri, Wes. It's good to be here under less stressful circumstances than last week. Hey, I want you guys to know we are leaving with a win this year."

Mike high fives his players as they strut across the court putting their stuff on the bench. He joins them encouraging them and drawing on his clipboard.

I bounce the balls over to some of their players as two girls from Wagon Wheel come by me. The first girl catches William's attention and then runs and jumps straight into his arms giving him a huge policy breaking kiss. All the kids love it and begin cheering even more loudly now. The second girl is wearing one of our staff sweatshirts; she tugs on it as she shyly walks toward John. They too embrace. They aren't near as close as the other two, but there's chemistry, or maybe history, and obviously a present because she's wearing his sweatshirt! I'm immediately reminded of Andee's words in the office about girls from Wagon Wheel. For the first time, I wonder if I have this all wrong.

Pete and Mark also hug these two Wagon Wheel girls and then a few other girls come on the court all hugging the guys. The girl with William sits on our bench and begins clapping and cheering for our team. I look across to see Marcie abruptly get up from the scorer's table and pushes her way through the cheering crowd. Laney follows after her. Andee stands on the corner of the court writing on her clipboard. Her smirk slays me.

56.

"Boys, great win tonight," I yell. "William, you are an amazing player. You carried me the entire game!"

The guys are congratulated by kids and staffers from both camps. Streams of toilet paper are all over the court. William and John talk trash with a few guys from Wagon Wheel before they go up to the buses. I look for the girls from earlier, but don't see them.

"Guys, let's celebrate the win. What do you say I bring up some snacks to the picnic table tonight? I'd like to talk with you about a few things. I'll come up a few minutes before curfew. That way you have time with your kids."

Mark's wiping his glasses, "Sure! Sounds great."

"I'm always up to celebrate," William says proudly.

They head up the dirt road together waving at the bus as it pulls out.

As the bus drives up the dirt road, a car comes the opposite way.

It stops near the guys. The lights are so bright on the car I can hardly make out what's going on. I squint to see John lean down and say something to his camper. The boy looks up at him and then at the car and then jogs toward the cabins. I start toward them as John turns toward the other guys as they all wave at the driver. Mark waves at John, leaving him next to the car. The passenger side door opens and John leans toward it, and then gets in the car.

The car comes toward me and slows. The driver's window rolls down as I make way to it. A strong British accent comes from the dark car, "Hello, Wesley Johnson, excuse me, 'Pastor' Wesley Johnson."

"Oh, hello, Pat. Good to see you."

"Is it?"

I glance at John. He's looking out the window as if he'd rather be anywhere in the world.

"You didn't call me back. My son didn't call me back so I decided to come here and talk with him myself."

"I see, but you only called yesterday?"

"Yes, I did. And you didn't return my call. So here I am. I came all the way from Los Angeles to see my son."

"Why don't you park and come up to our cabin. I know Sheri will be pleased to see you."

"Pardon me? I'm not here to talk with you or Sheri. If John's father were here to handle this I'm sure he would want to talk with you and you him, but obviously, he doesn't care about his son the way I do, so I am here to sort this out. Now, if you'll excuse me I'd like to talk with my son."

"Yes, that's fine. I think it would be better if we..."

She interrupts. "Oh, you think it would be better. You know what's better for my son, do you?"

John turns toward Pat and speaks to her as if I'm a ghost, "Mom, come on. He's only trying to be kind. Let's park and go sit on the bridge. The creek used to be your favorite spot. Come on, pull up there and park." She nods victoriously, never looking at me, winding up the window as they drive off.

I pray as I pack a bag of snacks in the canteen. I remember the story of the ten plagues where things were so dark that the Egyptians "felt" the darkness. That's what this feels like. This is dark.

It's right at curfew as I walk up to the cabins. John's campers must be going nuts without him.

When I arrive, I see things are surprisingly quiet, even in John's cabin. I set the snacks down on the picnic table and see Pete coming out of John's cabin.

"Hey Pastor Wes. We're all cool up here. See you in a second."

I wave back at him and sit down.

After a few minutes, the lights begin to go out in the cabins. Pete comes out and jogs over to John's cabin. A few moments later and the lights go out there too. All three guys converge at the table.

William speaks smugly, "Our victory party, huh?" He grabs a candy bar and a can of Coke.

"Something like that. I was hoping to talk with all of four of you, but I'm not sure when John will be coming."

"That's okay. He can handle it," Mark says.

William looks at the other guys and crushing his can he says, "But can we handle Pastor Wes? That's the question."

"Guys, I've been wanting to talk with you again since our meeting in the office last week. There's a lot I'd like to talk about, but after the basketball game and seeing those girls from Wagon Wheel, I can't help but wonder if I've gotten all of this wrong. I've chosen to believe you guys but after seeing those two girls at the game, I'm starting to think you guys might be playing me."

William motions to Mark, "Let me handle this." Mark sits back. "You mean the kiss and everything? I mean, I did carry you guys." He laughs at himself. The other guys sit tight as he continues, "What do you want to know Pastor Wes? Let's lay it all out. You know that's the way we roll."

"Okay. Let's start with the girl at the game, William. You obviously know her. You all know her and all the other girls too. Do you want to explain that?"

William turns over his guitar laying it in his lap, "Explain what? Just ask us what you want to know."

"I want to know how you know them. I want to know about the party last summer. I want to know about the accusation of you and John being out in the canyon earlier this summer. I want to know the truth. I want to know if I can trust you guys. And, I want to know it now. That's what I want."

Mark is nodding his head. He's clearly crafting his response as I'm talking. He waves toward the guys, "We're hearing you, Pastor Wes. Let's start with the party last summer with the Wagon Wheel staff. Yes, they hosted a summer's end party.

Most of the girls you saw tonight were there. We've known those girls awhile. Will and John are close to a couple of the girls, obviously Will more so." William wants to say something, Pete shakes him off.

Mark continues, "All four of us met up with them on a break day earlier this summer and we all hiked Squaw Peak. That's where the sweatshirt comes in. And yes, there was drinking in the park at the party last summer. Yes, Jenny Brown got drunk and passed out. To be honest, it was Will and John that pulled her out of the middle of that mess, things could have been so much worse. Pete and I got her back to her cabin and made sure she was safe. Her parents ended up taking her to the hospital. It was a nightmare."

"I can't imagine." I'd heard rumors about it all. And knowing how the Browns left the ministry, my heart hurts even more for them. They're such good people. "Thanks for taking care of her."

Pete leans in and says, "We'd do it for anyone, not just her."

"I want to believe you would. Were you guys drinking?"

Pete looks toward Mark and back at me. With real seriousness he says, "We told you back in the office that we didn't drink that night."

"You did tell me that, Pete. It's important to me that I ask. What else happened at the party?"

They all take quick glances at each other. William sits up, still animated. "It was a typical party. You know."

"No. I don't know, William."

"What's the word Mark, 'debauchery?' I think that's the best way to put it." He sneers.

Mark nods at William and then sits up straight. "A couple of the girls, the ones on the basketball court tonight, invited us to the party. We were the last ones to get out to the canyon. We brought some drinks and candy from the canteen. John invited Jenny along at the last minute. John and Jenny were close, still are close actually. Besides Jenny, we were the only ones from our staff out there. As you know, Andee was the one that eventually broke up the party.

William interrupts, "You probably know this too, but Andee appointed herself Jenny's Savior…I mean mentor. Mentor. Andee blamed us for everything. She totally blamed John for everything. She's been on him and us ever since."

"That's right," Pete says quickly. "We were actually trying to help."

"Go on," I say.

Mark smoothly adjusts his glasses and goes back to the story, "Yes, most of the staff from the Wheel were there. It was their party. A typical party, a big bonfire, music on the boom box, kids dancing, making out, and lots of drinking and smoking. Regardless of the accusations made against us, none of us were getting into serious trouble that night."

I sigh as I say, "What about Jenny? Tell me what happened to her."

Pete lowers his head. Mark looks straight at me, "Jenny was drinking with some of the other guys from the Wheel. Honestly, we hadn't been paying much attention cause we were talking with the girls. But then Jenny passed out and everybody started to freak out. John went over and tried to help her. He lifted her up trying to be sure she was going to be okay."

I shake my head. "This is heartbreaking to hear, Mark."

"I know, we all carry the guilt of that night."

"Doesn't sound like it was your fault…what happened after that?

William starts waving his hands, "Let me tell you straight – the way it happened. It was like this, the guys from the Wheel were being jerks all night. They didn't like it that their girls were hanging with John and me. When Jenny passed out and John went into their little circle to help her, those guys tried to stop him. John forced his way through…I helped him a little of course. John got Jenny to these two, and he and I ended up in a little fight with those punks. Pete and Mark got Jenny back to her cabin and John and I handled ourselves just fine with those posers. Just like tonight on the court."

"Okay, William, I think I understand." As we are talking we hear Pat's car coming up the road. "Hold on a second guys, I want to keep this conversation going. I'll be right back."

I wave as the car comes toward us. Pat slows and stops and then forcefully winds the window down.

"You won't need to worry another moment about my son. You'll have no more trouble, no disrespect from him for the rest of the summer. I assure you. I've dropped him off at the chapel. I told him he needs to get himself right with God." She winds up her window and drives away. I watch her as she passes the turn for the parking lot and heads toward the front gate. I shake my head as I realize that was it. She's headed back to L.A. Just like that.

I turn back toward the table and see the guys talking to each other. As I walk back I can see their conversation looks pretty intense. I stand at the edge of the table, "You guys have something else to say?"

"We've said a lot, maybe too much. But what else would you like to know?" Mark says.

It's as if they know exactly what is going on, not only in this conversation, but more importantly with the conversations we are not having.

I lean in and place both hands on the end of the table, "I want to know more about that party. But I really want to make sure John is okay. So, one last question, 'can I trust you guys?'"

William speaks first, "You can always trust these two guys. John too."

"I'd trust John, Mark and Will with my life," Pete says.

"I'm trusting all of you, including you, William. You need to let me know what I need to know and what you don't think I need to know. Understood?"

"Understood, Pastor Wes," William says. "Thanks for the talk. Good talk."

Mark speaks with a tone of gratefulness, "Thanks for checking on John."

<h1 style="text-align:center">57.</h1>

Sheri and I are talking with some girls while we wait on Andee to give us the okay to start the hike, when John comes over.

"Hey Pastor Wes. You have a sec?"

"Of course." I lean over to Sheri and the girls, "Excuse me for a moment." I step toward John. "What's on your mind?"

"I wanted to say sorry about last night…my mom and everything."

"You don't have to apologize. I am sorry. I should have called your mom back. Hey, I looked for you in the Chapel after your mom left but didn't see you."

"Oh, that's cool. It was late so I left…anyway, I know better. I should have called her."

"Listen, John. At some point, I'd like to talk with you about all of this. And, if you are up for it, I'd like to talk to you about anything else. I get the feeling there is more going on."

Laney walks up with a couple of girls, each holding their flashlights, "Hey Pastor Wes, a couple of my girls wanted to say hello to you." She slips her arm through John's arm and points to the girls, "This is April and Melanie."

"Good to meet you girls."

"You girls wanted to share something with Pastor Wes?"

April squints, "I want you to know we like what you're teaching us. 'You lack nothing'. Every girl like me has a list of things we lack."

Melanie nods, "If I could believe I really lack nothing, everything would change."

I look each girl in the eyes, "It's true. You lack nothing. Your counselor, and John here too. Even me. We lack nothing. No matter how hard it seems to believe."

Laney hugs Melanie, "Thanks girls. That was brave. It takes even more courage to live, doesn't it?"

I reach out and touch Laney's shoulder, "That's the greatest challenge, Laney, for all of us." The two girls smile, one hugs Sheri and then they quickly walk away. Sheri stretches her arm toward Laney. Their hands lock before Laney follows the girls.

"Sorry, again Pastor Wes," John says as he turns away.

I reach for him, "It's fine, John. Really. Listen, while you are here why don't you and Laney lead the Hike with Sheri and me tonight?"

"Oh, that's cool but we can't. We kind of hooked up a bunch of kids so we need to make sure they don't get too crazy once it gets dark."

"I see. Maybe next camp."

"Sounds great."

"Thanks, Pastor Wes," he says as he turns back toward Laney and the crowd of kids excitedly waiting for the Hike to begin.

58.

Andee runs through the statistics. There's less enthusiasm in this meeting than in any of the others we've had all summer. Maybe it's because the whole kitchen crew is mandated to stay at camp over the break. It's the biggest form of punishment we can level. Although it feels like a bit of a punishment for Sheri and me, as now we'll have to be here during the break. We could really use a break too, but we'll make the best of it.

I look at Andee. She doesn't look at me anymore. We've lost whatever partnership we had when the summer began. It wears me out to think she's been here all these years and is still the same person. I wonder if she's seen the change in me.

Without looking at me she says, "I'm sure Pastor Wes wants to say a few things. Let's hear it for Pastor Wes." A few claps and whistles welcome me.

My first thought is to bless this staff, put my hands on them one at a time, looking each one in the eye and tell them again, "You lack nothing." But then I look at Andee and choose to placate her. "This is our last break of the summer. There's like 12 days before the next time we are off, and that's the end of the summer, so please get some rest. In fact, if you want to stay here for the break we'll cook steaks and open the pool for a moonlight swim. We'll even do a big bonfire and make s'mores. We'd love to have you stay."

I notice William immediately shaking his head "no." He leans over and whispers something to John. A few others whisper back and forth. "Think about it and let us know if you'd like to stay. We'd love to have you."

I ask Sheri to lead us in our closing prayer. She smiles at me and stands, asking us to stand with her and grab hands. She prays about God restoring our strength, giving us courage. As she prays I hear the courage in her voice, a strength. The more she prays the more I'm strengthened. She closes by saying, "Remind us we lack nothing. Amen."

"Amen." I say. "Okay, family. Let's allow God to do exactly what Sheri just prayed. Let's live that truth. I'd like to see the kitchen staff. Everyone else is dismissed." The kitchen staff groan and slowly circle up around me. They know the talk I'm about to give them. Instead I bless. I speak to them all as gracefully as I can, and then I speak to them one at a time, "You lack nothing."

"Brian, you lack nothing…Marilyn, you lack nothing." A tear runs down her cheek. "Jennifer, you lack nothing." And around the circle. More tears, and a lot of smiles. An innocence lost or forgotten is being rediscovered as they begin to hug each other.

Laney and Sheri are talking in the corner. Sheri leans in toward Laney and they both quietly laugh. I always love to see Sheri smile. It's so good for her, and for me. My heart takes on an even bigger smile.

The boys from the kitchen ask about a basketball game. I wave toward Sheri and Laney and go down on the court to shag balls for the boys. I'm feeling much more alive. Those last moments were so rich, so right.

A few minutes later Sheri and Laney come out. John, who had been on the wall with Mark and Phoebe, get up to meet them. Then the two couples hold hands as they walk up the hill toward the cabins. Sheri walks down to the basketball court and leans up against the pole. She smiles and says, "You showing these boys you lack nothing on the court babe?"

"Yep. I'm going to show these rookies how it's done."

PART FOUR - JOHN

"Hey guys, so, slight change of plans. I'm not going to Phoenix. I'm staying here," Will says as we are walking back up to the cabins.

I immediately protest, "Wait. What? No way, Will. This is our last break."

"I know we all talked about going together, but I'm not going. You guys go and have a good time. Say hey to Ms. Audrey for me, John Lennon."

Pete shakes his head, "Hold on. What's going on, Will? Why would you want to stay around here?"

"Is it the stuff with Marcie?" Mark asks.

"Nah, I mean she was up for going, but I told her I was going to stay here."

Mark thinks he's tracking, "Oh, so you're staying to patch things up with Marcie?"

Will gets that cocky smile on his face. The one that is revealingly devious. Whatever is said with that smile is always entertaining. We all loosen up a bit. He leans in for dramatic effect, "Guys, today is 'Wednesday.'"

The other guys look at him unknowing. Marks asks, "Wednesday?"

"How do you even know what day it is out here?" Pete says.

I know exactly what's going on. "Dang, Will. You crack me up. Seriously?"

He nods and the cocky smile grows into a full-blown deviant smile.

The other guys are trying to put it together. Mark comes to it first. He slaps Pete on the arm, "Oh, man. It's Wednesday, Pete. It's the day girls from the Wheel do their weekly campout in the canyon."

Pete shakes his head. "Will, you're not going out there tonight, are you?" His voice quietly cracks.

"…Not exactly." He does his smile again.

"Sandy's coming here tonight. Isn't she?" I say, already knowing the answer.

He leans in again and whispers, "It's Wednesday night boys."

"You've got Marcie up there waiting on you, and you're up here waiting on Sandy? Are you sure about this?"

Mark looks at each of us and then says to Will, "I trust you, you know I do. But if anyone gets a glimpse of Sandy up here, anywhere near here, that'll be the end for all of us."

Will brushes him off, "You guys go. It's fine. It'll be awesome." He motions toward the girls as they're walking up. "Go play nice."

The girls are laughing together as we all look their way. Pete signals to the girls that we need a second. He steps a little closer to Will, "Look, Will, if you're staying, we are staying."

"No, you're not staying. I don't need you babysitting me."

I try again, "Come on, Will. Just come with us."

"Guys, seriously. You are not staying, and I'm not going."

Pete turns to the girls with the most defiant tone he can muster and says, "Girls, we're thinking about staying here for the break. Maybe going on a sunset hike."

Mark follows Pete, "And then tonight we thought we'd join the bonfire with s'mores and stuff."

Laney looks at me. She knows this isn't the plan. She knows how excited I am to introduce her to Ms. Audrey. I nod at her. She smiles back at me, looks at Will and then back at me and says, "Sounds great. I'm up for a hike."

"You guys…alright Sweet Pete. A hike through the canyon for everyone," Will declares.

"I guess if we aren't leaving, we won't need all of this stuff," Beth says as she picks up her backpack. "Let's go put it back in our rooms, girls. Meet you guys in an hour. Sound good?"

"An hour is perfect," Pete says as he reaches for Beth.

"Can't wait," Laney says.

We watch the girls for a second and then Will says, "You three are crazy. Sandy is still going to come, you do know that right? And, Sloop John B, seeing as you're going to stay we may as well get Joanna to come over too."

I smack him and say, "Don't even think about it, Will."

He brushes it all off, "Let's go play some hoops before your girls come back with their wedding dresses on."

As we come to the court we see the kitchen staff and Pastor Wes playing. He's as surprised to see us as we are him. "Hey, Pastor Wes!" Will yells. "We are staying here for the break. You got extra steaks?"

"Sure," he yells back. "You guys are staying?"

"Yep. We are. We had a change of plans."

"Oh, great. Let's get a big game going now and then we'll have a big appetite for dinner." He's enthusiastic in every way. He thinks we are moving toward him. He has no idea we are playing him. After all he's done for us, we are playing him. God, this is so very wrong. Even Will knows it. He doesn't know what to do with it, but he feels it. He shrugs and runs down the court.

60.

We decide to follow the creek as far as we can go. With Will deciding to stay and play ball, it's just the three couples. Soon it's only Laney and me. We've talked a lot over the last week or so, but there's so much about her I still want to learn.

"John, you haven't told me much about your parents. You talk a lot about Davis, but you really haven't said much about them. I know they're divorced."

"Davis is my hero, Laney. He's put up with so much b.s."

I look at her. I want her to really know. And the way she looks at me makes me think she really wants to know.

She thinks it's my family. I hate she thinks it's all about my parents, but some of this stuff I've never shared with anyone, not even God. She slips her arm in my arm as we walk. I try and take a step toward it, "Sure, Laney. What do you want to know?"

"Tell me about your mom."

"My mom…okay. Did you know she came out here the other night?"

"What? Here to camp?"

"She showed up the other night after the basketball game. She wanted to remind me of my mistakes and the consequences of those mistakes, and she wanted to remind me of…" I stop.

"Of what, John?"

"Of shame, Laney. She wanted to remind me of shame."

She stops and looks up at me. She brushes the hair out of my eyes, "I'm so sorry, John."

I pull her in with both arms, holding her tight.

"Laney, my mom is a lot, and I'd really like to blame her for my baggage, but the truth is I've really been an ass and hurt a lot of people too."

She pulls back and looks in my eyes, "I trust you."

"Laney, you hardly know me. I'm not sure how you can trust me. I can't trust me."

61.

Laney pulls a leaf off of the tree as we walk along the creek bank. She peels it along the veins.

I point across the way, "Check this out. The rain has widened this part of the creek. I love stuff like this. You up for hanging here for a minute?"

"Sure. How about that rock up there?" We climb up the rock and sit next to each other, dangling our legs over the side."

I point across her, "This is really cool. Check out the way the creek is flowing over that group of rocks."

She slips her arm through mine, "You get excited about the most interesting things."

"You think? Like what?"

She lifts her head toward the sky. "Well like this, like the way you watch the creek flow." She looks back at me holding my arm tighter, "Like the other day when you were talking about the funny smell."

"Oh, the smell after the first rain of the summer…that was so awesome, wasn't it?"

"Yes, it's so sweet. John, you have this strong, confident, cool surfer thing going on, but you have a soft side too."

"A soft side? Now you're making me nervous. Is that a good thing, or…" She smiles. Her smile puts me at ease.

She looks around and then back at me, "Can I ask you another question?"

"Sure, I'll be ready to give you a macho answer."

"Funny. I don't need that. I've had that." She tilts her head toward me. "It's your tenderness, John. That's what's so attractive."

"Tenderness is attractive. Okay. I dig it." I look at her and then shake my head, "But I have no idea what you're talking about."

She rests her hand on my leg, "Well, like the way you are with your campers, and your friends. Like the way you are with me, right here."

I scramble for something to say.

"So here's my question. What is it really that you like about being out here?"

"Geez, Laney. I don't know. I guess I like it out here because it's always peaceful. When I was a kid being out here was the only place it was quiet. My mom and dad were always at it. Our house was never quiet." I look at her again and then take a step toward the deeper stuff, "There's a lot in me that's not quiet. Out here even that stuff is a little more peaceful."

I put my arm around her and she leans in against me. My body begins to respond to hers.

She slowly speaks toward the creek, her head never moving from my shoulder, "Do you think this peace is big enough to hold all that is not at peace?"

"I guess so. I guess that's what's cool out here. It's not that all the darkness has somehow miraculously vanished or something. It's like, out here, you can bring all of it with you, but it doesn't win. You know?"

"I get that. I like that. So do you think God might be out here? In this peace?"

"When I was a kid, for sure, I thought God was out here." I look over her shoulder toward her eyes. "But I don't know anymore," my voice sounding more hesitant than I want it to be. It causes her to look up, looking at me in the eyes.

"What don't you know, John?"

"I don't know…"

"What?"

"I don't know how to be honest…"

"What do you mean?"

"I mean…I don't know what makes this peaceful. I don't know if God is out here or even up there. I don't think I've ever met God in church. I know where He isn't. I know that much."

"That sounds honest."

We sit in the quiet, or maybe this is peace.

"Keep talking, John."

I laugh a little and she laughs a little.

"I've always gone to church. I guess I've always wanted to believe in God, but it's not worked out the way I thought it would, or thought it should…I don't know if that even makes sense."

"It does make sense. It makes a lot of sense." She looks at me and tears well up in her eyes. "I remember my sister calling one Sunday night from Clemson asking me what I learned at church that day. I said, 'I'm learning how to hate myself.' I had no idea where it came from, it just came out. It was so true."

"God. I'm so sorry."

She doesn't say anything although it feels likes she wants to say more. She waits on me.

"After everything that's happened, I've never been able to get my act together enough for God to be okay with me. No matter what I did, or how much I tried. I'd do okay for a while and then something deep inside of me would get bumped, like a place in me that was already bruised, would get touched and then it would be a slippery slope and I'd end up throwing my hands in the air and saying 'to hell with it.'"

She turns her head toward me looking, up at me, "That's pretty tender, right there."

"That's almost as tender as it gets."

She pulls all the way up and looks inside me. I wonder what she can see. She says, "You know you can kiss me. I appreciate you being respectful. It's okay."

She leans toward me and we kiss. I stop and push back. Her eyes are still closed. She smiles before she opens them.

I whisper, "Because we're sitting in church right now, I have to be honest. If we start this, I'm going to have a very hard time stopping this."

"I'll stop you when you need to be stopped. We're not there yet."

62.

Sparks fly into the night sky from the bonfire as we walk up hand in hand. Pastor Wes is roasting marshmallows and handing them to Mrs. Johnson to make s'mores.

"Come grab the world's great late-night snack," Mrs. Johnson yells.

The staff gather around and devour everything in sight.

"Hey Laney," Mrs. Johnson yells. "Come help."

"Sure thing."

As she walks away Will comes over and in almost a whisper says, "Don't freak out on me right now John Coltrane, but just a heads up. Joanna is probably going to come over tonight with Sandy."

"Are you insane! Laney and I were just making out and you invited Joanna here! What are you doing?"

"Okay, hold on before you go all John Rambo on me. I mentioned to her that you guys decided to stay and she asked about you, that's all. I didn't invite her. I didn't tell her you were making out with Ivy League or Mark was drooling over Phoebe Cates."

I look back at Laney. She and Mrs. Johnson are working hard to keep the snacks coming. "Did you go out there earlier?"

"Yep, when you guys went on your love walk."

"Will…"

"Chill, no one saw me. I know how to hide. Listen, will you be cool to Joanna if she comes out here?"

"Will! What about Laney? I'm going to need to say something. There's no way I'm going to mess this up with her."

"That's fine. Tell her the girl you've been sneaking out with all summer is coming out here tonight."

"God, Will."

"Please, John Prine."

That breaks me a little, "John Prine. Oh, my God. 'Angel from Montgomery' is one of my mom's favorites."

"That's perfect, because it's one of Joanna's favorites too."

"Will!"

"I'm kidding. I'm kidding. Okay." He puts his guitar down and rests it on his leg. "If she does comes out tonight will you at least entertain her so I can have some time with Sandy? This is probably the last time I'll get to see her until after the summer."

"This the dumbest idea ever. You know that, right?"

"Please?"

"Okay. Just don't get crazy. Please."

Laney comes over and brushes my arm with her arm and smiles at me. She's wiping her the marshmallows off her fingers. She's seen some of what's happened between Will and I, but the cool thing is she doesn't ask me about it.

Pastor Wes yells, "10-minutes to curfew. Come get the world's greatest s'mores which will help you get the best night sleep of your life!"

We walk back and Laney hands me a s'more, "It's not pie, but it's close."

I down the whole thing and then ask, "You okay about today?

"I'm great. You okay?"

"Oh, my gosh. Are you kidding me? I got to make out with you in church."

<h1 style="text-align:center">63.</h1>

The after-curfew party is getting started as I walk up. Will is doing his best to play and sing quietly. He and Mark are singing Mötley Crüe's "She's Got the Looks that Kill." He nods for me to join them. We sing the chorus together banging our heads in true heavy metal fashion. Pete sits down and air drums as we make a big finish.

Will hands me his guitar, puts the pick in his mouth, and pulls his hair back into a ponytail. "Okay, guys I'm heading out."

"Heading out? You're going out there?" I say. "I thought Sandy was coming up here?"

"She was going to come, Joanna too, but I've thought about it. I'm going out there. It's better this way."

Mark says, "We'll wait here until you get back. Just to be sure everything is cool."

"Everything is cool. You guys don't need to wait up for me. Go to bed and dream about your girlfriends. You know you want to dream about mine." He gets up and walks toward the darkness. The three of us look at each other, not sure what to do.

I strum a few chords on Will's guitar while Mark sets up a board game. We've been playing awhile when we hear noises from the dirt road.

"Busted! We caught you out after curfew," Sandy says raucously as she and Joanna come into sight.

Mark jumps up.

"Hey John," Joanna yells. "Happy to see me?"

"Hey Joanna," I say.

"Hello girls," Mark says softly, "What's up? Where's Will? Is he with you guys?"

"What do you mean with 'you guys'?" Sandy slurs. Even from here I can smell the alcohol.

"This is bad," I whisper as I put Will's guitar in the case.

Joanna walks toward me. She's not as far gone as Sandy, but not far behind. Last time she was out here she had such an effect on me. Seeing her like this makes me feel sorry for her. God, I feel so judgmental all of a sudden.

Sandy stumbles and throws her arm around Mark.

"Whatcha playing, Choir Boys?" she says. "We want to play with you. Where's Will?" She lunges toward the game on the table.

Mark grabs her and steadies her, "Whoa. Sandy. Will's not here. We thought he was with you. Catch your breath and then let's get you back to the canyon."

Joanna follows, "I want to play with you, John. Do you want to play?"

"No, he doesn't," Pete says. "Will went out to your campsite. You guys didn't see him?"

Sandy points at the table, "We were supposed to meet him here. It's Wednesday." She puts both hands on the table, whines, and convulses, "I think I'm going to be sick." She takes a sip of Coke from the can on the table. "Oh, God. I'm going to puke."

Pete grabs her, "There's a bathroom right there in my cabin. Let me get you inside."

"No, I'll take her," Joanna says. She looks back at me. "I need to help her. This was my idea. It was all my idea. I wanted to see you, John." She starts crying and now I think she may be sick too.

I reach for her, "Okay, okay, let me help you."

Pete leads Sandy toward the cabin. Joanna and I follow.

I look over my shoulder at Mark. He's nodding nervously. His face is flushed, shoulders sunken. I've never seen him look like this.

Sandy is groaning as she walks into the stall. Once inside we hear her throw up. That sound has a universal effect, and sure enough Joanna runs into the next stall and throws up. If this weren't such a mess Pete and I might be laughing right now, but this is awful.

The stall door swings open and Sandy stumbles toward the sink. Pete runs back to his room to grab a few towels. I start the faucet for Sandy as she groans. Joanna comes out crying as she wipes her mouth with the sleeve of my sweatshirt. Sandy is staring at herself in the mirror with the faucet running. Pete hands Sandy a towel; Joanna has both hands on the sink like she's holding on to it for dear life.

A few minutes later Pete motions toward the door, "Okay, girls. You ready to head back? You'll feel better if you lay down."

We open the door to see Pastor Wes sitting down at the table next to Mark. There's a cooler and a bunch of candy on the table in front of him. He drops his head into his hands.

"Hey, look. It's Pastor Wes," Sandy yells. "Have you seen Will? He didn't…"

Pete interrupts, "Okay, Sandy. Let's get you back to your campsite."

Pastor Wes lifts his head and looks at Mark, "Where's Will?"

"He's not here," Mark says in complete defeat.

Tears begin to form in Pastor Wes' eyes as he looks at the four of us coming out of the cabin. He's putting it all together as he stands and pushes up his sleeves on his sweatshirt. He holds back his tears, "I'll take these girls back to the canyon and I'll clean this up. You get to your cabins. It's past curfew. We'll talk in the morning."

As I start to walk back I can hear the first sound of him crying.

64.

Mrs. Johnson's voice cracks over the loudspeaker, waking me, "Morning staff. Please report directly to your groups. One change this morning. Everyone will meet in their usual locations, except the Guy counselors. Guy counselors will meet with us, the Johnsons, in our cabin. Thank you."

This totally sucks. I drag myself to the shower to try and quench the smell of vomit that's only in my head.

Mark comes barreling in, "Dude, what was that? Think it's over?"

"Come on, Mark. Even you know it's over. I say we pack our stuff, go get the girls and make a run for it."

"I know you're only half joking. I'm with you, we're in serious trouble. Let's go get the other guys and make the best of it."

"Hey, Mark. Can I tell you something real quick?" I say as I slip on my flip flops. "I know this is a stupid thing to bring up right now, but I haven't been in that cabin since the night my parents split up."

"Oh, wow. I never even thought about that. I'm sorry, John."

"It's cool. It's just weird and now this?"

"You wanna talk about it?"

"I just did. Thanks. Let's get the guys."

As we head outside Pete is coming our way. "You guys ready for the firing squad?"

"I wanted to make an escape but Mark thinks it's best if we face it…Pete, where's Will?"

"He's not with you?"

"No," Mark says. "Did you check his cabin?"

"Went there first. He's not there."

"Pete, is his stuff there?" I ask nervously.

"I think so. His guitar is there."

"Oh, God." I look at both of them, "Please don't tell me he's still out in the canyon."

Pete shakes his head, "I waited up as long as I could."

"So did I. I was looking out the window," I say. "I never saw him or Pastor Wes."

Pete looks at Mark, "What do you think? What do we say?"

"Let's just be honest, like always," Mark says.

I shake my head. "I don't think honesty's going to help here."

Pete knocks on the door and Mrs. Johnson answers wiping her eyes, "Come in. You can sit at the kitchen table," she says, never looking at us.

The guys walk in ahead of me. It takes me a split second to choose to actually step across the threshold. I stop and look around. Everything looks like the same. Rembrandt's "*The Return of the Prodigal Son*" is still mounted over the fireplace. Same painting, different pain.

Mark looks at me and whispers, "You good, man?"

"I'm good."

Mrs. Johnson's Bible sits open on the table. She smooths the pages as she waits for us to each sit down. She starts talking as if she's rehearsed these lines.

"Boys do you have any idea what kind of trouble you are in? What kind of trouble we are in? Do you know the damage this can do to our camp? What about our reputation as pastors?" She points her finger at me, "John, you of all people should know better!"

I wince, but I'm not surprised this got put on me. Mark glances at me.

"Mrs. Johnson," he says, "Is Pastor Wes here, or…?"

She snaps back, "Don't pretend like you care about my husband after all you've done!"

Mark is taken aback.

"My husband has taken William to Wagon Wheel. They are going to report all that happened last night to the local authorities."

We sit stunned. Even Mark is lost. He rubs his hand through his hair. Pete sits up and says, "Mrs. Johnson. We are really confused. We know about the girls coming over here last night, but what does that have to do with Will and the authorities?"

She glares at him and sighs, "Pete, don't patronize me or Wesley."

Mark regains himself and takes over, "Mrs. Johnson, we only want to understand. What's going on with Pastor Wes and Will?"

"I think you boys have done enough." She looks at me whispers across the table, "I'm so disappointed in you, John. My husband believed in you. He fought for you. We both did. Now look at what you've done." I don't even look at the guys. I push my chair back and get up. Pete gets up and then Mark follows. "Go ahead, walk out! Dr. Hill said none of you would have the courage to face this."

I fire back past Pete and Mark, "Courage? This isn't about courage, Mrs. Johnson. This right here, is about being shamed!"

She starts crying burying her head in her hands. I turn toward the door.

She speaks through her tears, "You feel disrespected, what did you say, 'shamed?' You?! I don't even know how to respond to that. Sit down and wait for my husband."

Mark grabs me and looks at me sympathetically. He waves his arms, motioning for me to slow my roll. "I think I got it. Trust me." He nods toward the table.

I look at Mrs. Johnson whose head is in her hands and shake my head and whisper to Mark, "This is total bullsh*t."

Mark leads us back to the table. Pete mouths back to me, "Big time bullsh*t."

We all sit in it.

Mrs. Johnson abruptly pushes her chair back, stands, and begins to walk away.

Mark calls for her, "Mrs. Johnson…"

She turns back from the hallway. "You will wait here until my husband returns."

Mark turns back and closes her Bible, "This is bullsh*t."

Pete forces a grin and looks at Mark, "I thought you handled that pretty well, Mark. You almost had it." They try and laugh a little. Mark shakes his head in bewilderment. I'm smoldering.

They sit and wait for what will happen next. I sit and remember. I know what happens next.

65

"Give me a few minutes boys. I need to see my wife," Pastor Wes says as he walks past us, toward the bedroom, never looking at us.

We look out the window for Will but don't see him, our anxiousness reaching a new level.

Pastor Wes finally reemerges, Mrs. Johnson is behind him clutching a box of Kleenex and sits on the couch. She's wiping tears from her eyes, but the look on her face has changed. It's gone from full blown wrath to an ounce of sobriety. She even halfway smiles as she looks toward me. What the hell? So fake. Totally fake!

Pastor Wes sits at the table. His head is hung. He speaks from a place of defeat.

"William confessed to everything. I dropped him off at his room so he's packing now and then he'll come over here."

He starts telling a rambling story about his uncle or something. I tune him out.

I hate this house. There is nothing good about this house. It's here, sitting at this table, where my dad learned my mom was having an affair with their boss from headquarters, Mr. Terry. I knew it all along. I'd seen them together, but dad didn't have a clue. It was here, at this table, where dad told Davis and me that our mom was leaving. He said she was packing up her clothes and would come tell us goodbye. Then he went out for a walk. I got up to follow him and left Davis sitting alone at this table. In a fit of rage, anger, and desperation, my mom not only grabbed her clothes, but grabbed Davis. It was six months before I saw either of them again.

And it was here at this very table the summer before all that, where I told my parents what first happened to me in Quartzite. They didn't believe me. I've never said a word about it since. Even after it happened again and again. I can feel it all again, right here at this table.

Mark looks at us and then at Pastor Wes. He adjusts his glasses and says, "You mentioned Will's confession Pastor Wes. Can you tell us about that? What did he say?"

"Mark, I don't have the energy for all of this."

Pete looks at me and then Mark for understanding. I have no idea.

Mark tries again, "Pastor Wes, we really don't understand. What did Will do, or what did he say he did?"

"He said you guys didn't know about all he was doing. I find that hard to believe."

"We really aren't sure what happened," Mark says. "Obviously the girls from the Wheel were drinking. But Will didn't have anything to do with that."

For the first time Pastor Wes looks at us. He looks each of us in the eyes. I can see him battling to understand, maybe battling to believe. A glimpse of life comes across his face. He stands, "Okay, guys. Let's leave this here. This all stays here. Let me be very clear, you are not to talk about this with anyone outside of this room until we talk again. Is that clear?"

Mark looks at Pete and me. We stand in silent solidarity and then leave. As I close the door, we see Will's car turn up the dirt road toward the front gate. He's leaving without saying goodbye.

66.

These new campers deserve better than what I am giving. I've only learned a couple of names all day. At dinner I watch Laney with campers and can hear her laugh above all the noise. I'd give anything for a walk down the creek with her. I wouldn't say a word or I'd say every word. I don't know which.

67.

We get to the campfire pit early. I'm hoping Laney and her girls will be here early too. They aren't here. It's just us. I decide I have to get it together.

"Alright, huddle up boys. We have a few minutes to talk before Campfire. I want everyone to get to know each other. You guys are all from different parts of the desert, is that right?" They all nod. "Okay. Everybody is going to introduce themselves by telling us your name, where you're from, your favorite desert animal, or your favorite book, movie, or sports team, or something." They all look at each other and get either excited or nervous.

The conversation starts fast. I've got a few names down when I see Mark and his guys come our way. Mark is stopped by Andee at the bottom step. I try not to get distracted, but there's no way I can fully pay attention to these guys when Mark and Andee are talking. Mark doesn't seem defensive, he's got a kid hanging off him.

The kid across from me says his name. All I hear is his last name, Harris. "Did you say Harris?"

"Yes, Ellis Harris from Yuma."

"And what's your favorite book or team 'Ellis Harris from Yuma?'"

He tugs at his Magic Johnson jersey, "Lakers baby!"

"Ellis Harris from Yuma, Laker Showtime fan. That's rad, dude. I dig it." I look down and see Mark heading toward me. He smiles confidently and keeps walking. His guys sit behind mine. I hear him talking with his boys.

I look back at my guys, "Wait, did you say Charles Harris?"

"No, Ellis."

"Whoops. Sorry about that. Ellis/Charles Harris from Yuma, what grade are you in?"

"I'm in 8th grade."

"Awesome. Ellis/Charles Harris from Yuma, do you like to read? Please tell me you like to read."

"No, reading is for sissies. I said I'm a Laker fan."

"Oh, I see. Sissies." I look at the other guys, "Guys, this is no longer Ellis Harris from Yuma. His new nickname is 'Dill.' Just, 'Dill.'" Everybody laughs except Ellis Harris from Yuma.

I look back and call for Mark. He slides down and his guys follow. "Dill, I want you to meet Mark. This is one smart guy right here. He's going to be a lawyer when he grows up, he's already defending me and some other guys in a little battle we've got going on around here. We call him Mark, but you can call him, 'Atticus.' 'Atticus Finch.' Dill Harris meet Atticus Finch."

Mark reaches over and shakes his hand, "You have no idea what your nutty counselor is talking about do you?"

Dill shakes his head. Mark looks around at my guys and his, "Atticus Finch? Boo Radley? Anyone?" Mark points at me and says, "You guys better figure this one out. It's going to be a long camp with this guy unless someone gets this. I'm warning you."

I lean in, "I'll buy at the canteen tomorrow for the first person who can tell me about Atticus Finch and Dill Harris. I'll give you one more clue. Atticus has a daughter named Scout." They stare blankly at me. They have no idea. "Go. Go figure it out. You have three minutes. If no one has it figured in three minutes you're all buying for me and Mark at the canteen tomorrow!"

The guys from both groups scatter and are running around the campfire pit asking everyone who comes up about Atticus and Dill. It's actually kind of funny. I square around with Mark and ask him how it went with Andee. "Interesting," he says. "She was fishing for details. She obviously knows Will is gone, but that's it. I don't think the Johnsons have said anything else to her or to anyone."

"Not that we know anything either…other than Will is gone."

"It sucks. Totally sucks."

I see Marcie for the first time all day. She looks terrible. "Hey Mark, do you think Marcie is okay? Do you think she knows anything?"

"Definitely not okay. I don't think she knows much. If she knew the whole story she wouldn't be here."

A couple of my guys come running up the steps toward me, "'To Kill Lady-bird.' It's from a movie. 'To Kill the Ladybug, or Ladybird!'"

"Oh, please boys. Please. Come and sit down with me. You guys are embar-rassing me." I'm about to tell them the answer when I see Laney. I'm so glad to see her in this moment, more than any other. "Boys, listen. Let's do double or nothing. I'll bet you that girl right there knows the answer." They all look at her.

They shoot down the stairs and stop her. She laughs at them and puts a hand on the shoulder of one of my guys. "To Kill a Mockingbird," she says. Then she leans down and whispers in his ear.

They look back at me and yell, *To Kill a Mockingbird, To Kill a Mockingbird!*

I stand and applaud, "Yes, my young grasshoppers. Yes."

The boy with whom Laney was whispering comes running up to me, "That girl told me to ask you if you know if E. B. White is a boy or a girl."

"Oh, here we go," I yell toward her. "Jokes. She's got jokes! E.B. White is a guy, Charlotte!"

Laney's cracking up as she looks at me. She gets her girls to their seats as the music starts playing. My guys are all talking and laughing. I'm feeling an ounce better.

Mark slaps me on the back, "Remember it's a sin to kill a mockingbird."

"Thanks, Atticus. I remember everything about sins. The hardest part is to forget.'"

68.

As Pastor Wes gets up to speak all the life that has been flowing in me over the last hour begins to drain.

"I want to tell you about one of my favorite paintings. Some of you have a favorite basketball player, or superhero. I want to tell you about one of my favorite painters."

I start shaking my head. "You can't be serious," I whisper aloud.

"What's up, John?" Dill asks.

"Oh…nothing. Stop talking. Pay attention. You have a lot to learn." He smiles and leans in resting his elbows on his knees.

Mrs. Johnson comes up front carrying the painting from their cabin.

"Oh, that's cool," Dill whispers my way.

"It's Rembrandt. He used to play for the Lakers."

"He did? That's awesome."

"Would you be quiet and listen."

He smiles and reassumes his position.

As Pastor Wes begins, I whisper to Dill, "I bet you $20 I know where he's going with this."

"I don't have $20. I have $2. No bet. You've already got me twice tonight. Stop talking."

The story of *The Return of the Prodigal Son* was one of my dad's favorites. My mom bought him the Rembrandt painting for Christmas one year. He hung it in our cabin at camp. During the last week of every summer he'd bring down the painting from the cabin and tell the story while pointing out the characters in the painting. I used to love it. It was actually my favorite. There's nothing to love about what's happening right now. This is like a sucker punch.

Pastor Wes goes on to tell the story pretty close to the way my dad told it. "Where do you find yourself in the story?" he asks. When he finally sits down I literally exhale. I can't help but think about Will…and my dad. Man, how did stuff get so messed up? How did I get so messed up? Will it ever change? Any of it? Ever?

The line from *To Kill a Mockingbird* won't leave me. "Sometimes the Bible in the hand of one man is worse than a whiskey bottle in the hand of – oh, of your father."

69.

The first night in the cabin is always the hardest. Tonight we set up a wrestling ring, we have a pillow fight, and we even tell ghost stories. Finally, things start to settle down. As we are pushing the beds back in place one of the guys hits the lone mirror in our cabin with the corner of his bed frame. Glass shatters everywhere. Everyone freezes.

"Oh, sorry. My bad," he yells.

"It's cool. Hop up on your bed. We don't need any blood tonight. I'll clean it up," I say.

The guys begin to whisper to each other as I sweep up the glass and go back and forth to the outside trashcan. On my last trip out, I see Mrs. Johnson coming up the dirt road. I turn quickly to pretend I don't see her.

She waves, "Wonderful night, John. Everything okay?"

I glance over my shoulder and see her sit at the picnic table. Her presence there feels like betrayal. I choose not to say anything, nodding at her and coming back inside. I slip into my room and sit on my bed.

Quiet laughter and whispers begin to distract me from my temptation to descend further still. It's Dill.

"What's up Dill Harris?" I shout from my bed.

"Nothing, Scout!" he yells.

"Are you kidding me, Dill? Scout's a girl!" I get up and come out into the cabin. Dill is laughing. His laugh makes me laugh. The rest of the guys are laughing too.

I go back and grab *The Voyage of the Dawn Treader*. I've been reading this series aloud all summer. I've got these last three books to go before the end of this camp. I pull up my stool and sit next to the window, "Alright guys. It's story time." I open the book and flip to the first chapter. The chapter title knocks the wind out of me, "The Picture in the Bedroom."

70.

Days go by and not one word is said to the staff or to us about Will. Not one word. I hate it. I miss him. I hate being left.

<h1 style="text-align:center">71.</h1>

I've been fighting it all week but tonight, the darkness is covering the deepest parts of me. I have my book on my lap but don't read. I flip over the photograph I use as a bookmark, back and forth, while peeking out the window from time to time. My guys whisper until there's nothing left to whisper about. The room fills with the darkest kind of silence.

The more I sit here, the more my soul stirs. The secrets. The guilt. The shame. Damn, I fight this stuff every day. It's one thing to get into a fight at school because of a girl, or because some kid is being an ass, but how the hell do you fight shame?

I gotta get out of here before it takes me all the way down. I slip outside, not totally sure where to go or what to do. I glance over at Mark's cabin. All the lights are off. Pete's too.

If I was at home I'd go to Dawn's or go up to the 7-11 on the corner of Clark and Artesia. They don't check IDs there. But I'm not there. I'm here, again.

I walk toward the front gate. The thought of going to Joanna's brings an illicit comfort and an ache of desire.

Faces flash through my mind as I walk. My mom and Mr. Terry. Davis. Mrs. Johnson. Lonny. Him. All the hope that began to take hold through the summer has vanished. I don't know where it went.

I remember the conversation Laney and I had a while ago about saying something to her if I was in a dark place. If there was a time, it's now. But if I say something to her, at this time of night, she'll know I can't handle my sh*t.

The chapel is up the road. I decide to walk up that way. If someone catches me out here I'll make up an excuse about going up there to pray or something. I see a little light on inside. Seeing I'm up here I may as well go inside. The front door is locked so I wander toward the back door looking through the windows. The back door is locked, but not fully closed. I yank on the handle and the door opens. The light of the little lamp casts a shadow on the cross that adorns the fake stained glass. I sit in the seat where I normally sit and stare at the cross. I've been sitting in this seat all summer looking at this cross. I don't know what I'm looking for. I guess I'm hoping something is looking at me, or looking for me. I sit here awhile, staring. There's nothing. The only thing I find here is more silence. It's maddening.

I head down toward the girls' cabins. Things are as quiet up here as they're down by our cabins. Laney's is the last cabin on the dirt road. I lean up against the wall, trying to decide what she'll do if I knock, and what she'll say, and what I'll say. I knew I was coming here all along.

I tap on the window and call her name. More silence. I try again, this time I knock harder and call one more time, "Laney, you awake?"

"John. Is that you?"

"Yes."

She opens the door and immediately embraces me. I don't say anything.

She pulls back and puts both hands on my chest. I glance over her shoulder and see Marcie sleeping on the other side of the room. There's used tissues all over the floor.

Laney looks over, "She's come in here every night since Will left."

"Oh, man. Dang."

She brushes the hair out of my eyes, "What are you doing, is everything okay? Do you want to come in, or let me grab my sweatshirt and I'll come out?"

"No, no. It's cool. I'm good. You don't need to come out. I don't want to get you in trouble. I just wanted to see you for a second."

"John, what's going on?"

I look at Marcie, "Is she okay?"

"She's making it. What about you? What's going on?" She starts to pull away for her sweatshirt. I grab her before she can.

"It's okay. I'm good. I just couldn't sleep and thought if I walked for a while I'd settle down."

"You sure? I'll walk with you if you want."

One of the girls calls for her from inside the cabin.

Laney loudly whispers, "Be there in a sec."

"I better let you get to her."

"She'll be okay. Are you okay?"

She steps toward me and I wrap my arms around her. We are standing so close and yet the fear in me is so present. I back off. She's not moved. She says, "Hey, I know there's a lot of your story I don't know. And there's some of mine you don't know. But, I'm here. I'm with you. I'm not going anywhere."

"That's about the coolest thing I've ever heard."

"I mean it, John. I really do."

"I'd better go. Can I kiss you before I get out of here?"

"You can only kiss her if you come in here and kiss me too!" Marcie says from across the room.

I kiss Laney on the cheek. She puts her hand on my chest. Her face flickers a spark deep in me.

"Night, Marcie."

"Night, John," she says.

Laney stands at the door as I turn and wave.

I walk back through camp hearing the cicadas buzzing their moonlight song. The rustle in the ivy startles a few birds to find a new resting place. I stop on the bridge leaning over the rail to watch the water quietly smoothing the stones underneath.

72.

"That skit was hilarious, John," Pete says as we walk back up to the cabins after campfire. "When you moonwalked off the stage at the end, my guys went nuts!"

"It was all Mark's idea."

"Hey, I've got another idea," Mark says. "What if we all go to the beach at the end of the summer?"

"Let's do it," I say. "I bet the girls will be up for it. We could call Will and pick him up on the way to L.A."

"I'm in," Pete replies quickly. "You really think Ivy League would come, John?"

"I think so. That would be so insane. I'd love it…oh my God. Can you imagine my mom and Laney?"

"Ivy League can handle her." Pete points at me, "If she can handle you, she can handle your mom."

"Not even Laney can handle my mom, Pete." We all laugh in agreement.

"You know," Mark says, "If we camp out at the beach we call all avoid your mom!"

As we are standing in front of my cabin talking Mrs. Johnson comes up and sits at the picnic table. She's been sitting there the last couple of nights. She waves at us. The other guys wave back. She's been trying to be nice to us the last couple of days. I've ignored her. God. Her being at the table makes me sick to my stomach.

I can hear my guys whispering as I open the cabin door. They all dive on their beds as I walk in. "Everybody good?" I grab my book and pull up the stool in front of the window.

"Everybody ready for chapter 5?" There are some responses, mostly nervous laughter. Something is up. I flip through my book and glance out the window.

"Shhh, he'll come and take it away."

That's all I need to hear, "What are we hiding boys?"

"Nothing. Nothing to see here," Dill says. "Just an awesome painting."

I walk back and flip on the light, "Hand it over." All the guys sit up on their beds as nervous laughter floats across the room.

"Turn what over?" Dill says.

"I'm guessing one of you guys has a magazine that has some posters of some stuff that's fake."

The responses come again.

"He knows."

"Busted."

"What do you mean fake?"

I sit on the edge of Dill's bed and look across the room. "Pastor Wes' wife is outside at the picnic table. You guys have five seconds to hand it over or I'll walk out there and ask her to join me for this conversation about what's fake and what's real on this poster."

The quietest kid in our cabin, Billy, whose bed is in back corner, gets up and slowly comes toward me. He's definitely not laughing. He's terrified. I think he might burst into tears as he hands the *Playboy* to me.

"Billy!" Dill says.

"Is this yours?" I ask.

"It's my dad's. He'll kill me if he finds out I took it." Everyone but Billy starts laughing and carrying on. Billy is totally freaked out. I know the hurt that can be inflicted on him in this moment. God, I know it.

"Hey, it's okay. You're not in trouble, Billy. You're okay."

He turns and walks quickly back to his bed. That kid has a story, for sure.

I take the *Playboy* and walk outside and throw it in the trash can. The shattered glass vibrates as the magazine hits the bottom of the can.

"We are going to talk about sex this week guys. We aren't going to talk about it tonight. But we are going to talk about it. This is a big deal." I turn off the lights.

The snickering starts again in the other corner. "He said a big deal."

I grab a much safer topic in *Dawn Treader* and pull out my bookmark. I start reading aloud, "The Storm and What Came of It."

73.

The dirt road is crowded as we stumble toward breakfast. Mark is telling me and Vista about the beaches in South Carolina, "The locals say 'the tide is the heartbeat of the Lowcountry.'"

"That's deep, Mark," I say. "Have you ever done a grunion run?"

"No, but I've heard about it, how all the grunions swim end up on the beach at night or something?"

"Yep. It's a mating season thing. And you'll love this, the best runs are during full moons."

Pastor Wes pulls his car onto the road. He divides our crowd like Moses and the Red Sea. He motions toward me and rolls down his window. I look across at Mark. My heart hardens as I lean over toward the window.

He shades his eyes with his hand as he looks up at me, "Hey, John. Headed into headquarters." He smiles, "Your dad used to call it 'The Q.' You want to jump in and join me for the day?"

I see the file folder on the passenger seat, "William Simmons." He sees me notice it. He flinches and then looks back again at me, "What do you say?"

"No, thanks. We've got a busy day with this crew. Thanks for thinking of me."

He nods and then looks ahead. He puts both hands on the wheel and leans his head back against the head rest. He squints as he looks back at me, "Your dad took me with him to The Q one day. We had the best time."

"Oh, that's cool. Glad you had that time with him. Well, have a good day." I tap the top of his car and step back, "See you later." He nods and looks to the other side of the car, waving at a few kids as he pulls up the road.

<h1 style="text-align:center">74.</h1>

A few of my guys are talking about the Lakers when I catch up. They think because I'm from Los Angeles that I should be best friends with Magic Johnson. A yell from Dill shocks me.

"John, come back, quick! Billy is bleeding!" Dill is at the top of the hill waving. "John, it's bad! It's bad! He's dying!"

I glance at Mark and turn, running as I fast as I can toward the cabin. I jump over the lid to the trashcan and through the open door. There's a trail of blood leading to the back of the cabin. Billy's on his bed writhing in pain. He's holding a T-shirt against his hand that is soaked red. There's blood running down his hand.

I yell at Dill to get a towel as I try and calm Billy.

"Hey man, I've got you. Let me see."

"I'm sorry, John. I'm sorry," he says in between crying heaves. "I don't want to get into trouble…my dad…he'll kill me…if he finds out."

"Look at me, Billy…hey, it's okay. You're going to be okay."

Dill brings me a towel and leans over, almost in between Billy and I.

I hold Billy's hand while trying to pull the T-shirt from his hand. The closer to the cut, the louder Billy cries. Part of the T-shirt is stuck to a flap of skin. I quickly wrap the towel around the T-shirt.

"Dill, get me another towel."

Andee comes rushing in the front door. She's holding a handful of folders in her arm, "What's your name, young man?"

"Billy…Lane," he says as he gasps for breath and then screams.

She rifles through the folders, "Billy Lane from Buckeye?"

"Uh-huh," he groans through his sobs.

Andee is ripping through forms in his file.

Mrs. Johnson comes in rattled and nervous. She leans in and tries to comfort Billy. Her worried look continues to grow as she looks my way, "How bad is it?"

"His hand is falling off," Dill says. "Just look at it!" Billy screams again.

I move back in front of him to look at him in the eyes, "Hold on, dude. Hold on." He's writhing in pain. I wipe his face, "Your arm is not falling off, it's cut badly, very badly. We need to get you to the hospital."

Billy shrieks, "No, I can't go to the hospital…my dad…No."

Andee looks at him, "We need to get you there, son. You be brave. You'll be fine." She looks at Mrs. Johnson, "The nurse isn't here. She took the camp van into town to gather supplies."

"Then one of us will need to take him."

Billy screams, "John! John, you're going take care of me, right?"

Andee, still looking in the folder, says flatly, "He's not authorized to sign for you."

"No. John needs to come with me." He starts sobbing, "John."

I look at Andee and at Mrs. Johnson, "Can I just ride with you guys?" That's not what Andee wants to hear.

Mrs. Johnson looks at Andee and then at me. She nods toward me, "Okay, John. Go get your truck and we'll meet you at the office."

For a split second I'm totally stunned, then run up the dirt road as fast I can. I jump in the truck and am back down the dirt road stopping quickly in front of the them, causing dust to float across the road and over the office. Mrs. Johnson holds the folder under one arm and the other arm around Billy. Dill follows.

"You've got this, Billy." Dill says. I knew she wouldn't do it, but I was so hoping Mrs. Johnson would just let me take him. Instead, she closes the folder and gets in on the other side of the truck.

She looks at me with a worried expression, "You are not authorized to sign for him. Let's go. We need to hurry."

Dill waves goodbye as we speed toward the front gate.

The ride is miraculously quiet as Billy falls asleep. Mrs. Johnson keeps checking on Billy every few minutes.

"What happened back there, John?"

"What do you mean?

"How did all of this happen?"

"I'm not sure. I didn't ask him. I'm guessing he cut it on some broken glass."

She checks Billy again. "Obviously."

At the turn onto the highway Mrs. Johnson tries to make small talk. "So, how are things with Davis?"

"He's fine. Thanks." I look out the window and adjust the radio. Not that it would connect to any station out here.

"Just a lot of static there, huh John?"

"Yep. A whole lot of static," I mumble as I pop in my mom's John Prine cassette I stole from her right before I left. Mrs. Johnson stares out the window and hums along to "Angel from Montgomery." I never really listened to the words before. Man, it's sad. I guess that's why my mom liked it.

Four or five grueling hours later Billy leaves the hospital with 19 stiches, a heavy dose of medicine, guilt, and whole ton of shame as all the weight of what happened has overtaken him. He's hardly said a word. He's suffocating in it.

When we finally pull into the canyon Mrs. Johnson says, "Billy, your dad would like to talk with you when we get back to camp. I talked with him at the hospital to keep him informed. He's so glad you are well."

Billy tears up a little and looks at me shaking his head, "He's going to kill me."

"Hey, come on man. He's not going to kill you."

"You don't know him."

"I know something about parents who you think want to kill you. They really don't. They just have a weird way of showing love."

"I guess." He turns his arm back and forth looking at the bandage. "He's going to kill me."

All of a sudden, he starts talking. He tells me about his younger brother and I tell him about Davis. He talks about playing trumpet in the band at middle school. When I mention Maynard Ferguson who played the trumpet parts in the *Rocky* movies he comes alive like it's Christmas morning. We talk as if Mrs. Johnson isn't even in the truck, although she listens intently to every word.

"Hey, let's keep talking back in the cabin."

He nods almost excitedly, "Okay."

We stop at the office to call his dad. The life that was in Billy five minutes ago evaporates. He carries a curse passed down from his dad. I can see it in his eyes. That's a whole different kind of pain.

Mrs. Johnson opens the folder to find the phone number. Billy freezes. I interrupt, "Mrs. Johnson, is it cool if I call and say a quick hello to Mr. Lane, being Billy's counselor and all? Then, I'll pass the phone to you and Billy."

Billy is nodding. His despair is trying to give way to hope, "Can he, Mrs. Johnson?"

"Sure." She gives me the look, handing me the folder.

"Mr. Lane, this is John Cunningham. I'm the luckiest counselor out here at camp. I get the honor of hanging with your son. He's the coolest kid!"

Billy looks at me exactly the same way I looked at Mr. Reis back at Mayfair High. I do my best Mr. Reis interpretation as Billy's dad says he's really busy with a client and that this call is "terribly inconvenient" and he just wants to know the "bottom line."

"Yes, sir. Then I won't keep you. Hey, I want you to know that Billy's doing great and I've not seen such courage in a kid in a long time. He was strong through this whole thing. I'm totally proud of him. 19 stitches like a champ. He's the man!" A moment later I hang up. I smile at Billy. "He says, 'he's proud of you too.'"

Mrs. Johnson looks at the folder on her desk and nods at Billy, "We are going to need to fill out a report on this incident, Billy."

"Can we do that later, Mrs. Johnson?" I ask. I look over at Billy. "It's already been a long day."

"Sure, John. I'll get the details from you later."

"Great. Thanks. Let's find Dill and the guys," I say. Billy is beaming.

75.

I've gotten a few chances to talk with Laney since the other night. We've talked mostly about our kids and about how things are going with them. She's been really focused and engaged with Billy, which makes Dill jealous as I'm pretty sure he's in love with her.

I've hesitated saying anything about the end of the summer. Mississippi and Southern California couldn't be farther apart. She hasn't brought it up either. After the other night, I'm positive this isn't a summer fling for her, but I have no idea what happens after this.

I'm rebounding for some guys when Laney comes down on the court.

"Hey you. Looks like we get to be together for a couple of hours this afternoon. How did that happen?"

"I have no idea. This is totally rad. It's the first time we've been assigned together all summer!"

She laughs, "A total oversight on someone's part I'm sure."

I bounce the ball her way. She walks out onto the court like she owns it, "Let's get this game started." She splits the kids into teams, assigns them a basket, and looks at me and then looks at the kids. "Play ball!" she yells.

She and I jog to the bench on the side of the court. "Saved you a seat, coach!" I say. She slings her arm through mine and I pull her in. I lean on her a little, "That was pretty great. The way you did that, got all those kids going."

"I know a thing or two about basketball."

"Ya, it was all great until that part when you yelled, 'Play ball'."

She hangs her head and pulls her cap over her face, laughing at herself. "Shoot. Baseball. I know better."

"Yep. Baseball."

We yell and cheer as the kids play. Other kids come and join us on the benches as we clap and sing and make up funny cheers.

Andee's announcement over the loudspeaker ends the best two hours of the entire summer, for sure: "Attention campers and staff Free time is now over. Dinner will be served in 30 minutes."

The kids scurry to their cabins. Laney and I pick up the balls and throw them into the bag. "Laney, we make a good team, you and me."

"I think so."

She smiles at me. I don't need her smile, her presence is enough, but God her smile fills me. "Hey, have you ever been to Southern California?" I ask.

"No, I haven't. But it's every girl's dream who grows up in the Mississippi Delta. They play a little basketball there in L.A, the Los Angeles Lakers!"

"Oh, look at you! Well yes, they do. Why don't you come sometime? I'll take you to a game, I'll save you a seat."

"I'd like that." She smiles and waits.

I grab another ball and throw it in the bag. She has a ball under her arm and hands it to me.

"Do you have to go home as soon as camp ends or would you be up for coming to Southern Cal for a few days?"

She pauses and nods like she's figuring an answer to a math problem, "Will Davis be there? I'd get to meet him right, 'the person who loves you more than any other person on the planet?'"

"Yes, of course you'd meet Davis. That would be an absolute…that would also mean you'd probably have to meet my mom and Mr. Terry, and my dad and his wife Sue…but I think Pete and Mark might come, Will too hopefully, and maybe Beth and Phoebe, so it shouldn't be too painful."

She does her eyebrow raise thing, "In that case I'd love to come. Can't wait."

"Oh, awesome. So, awesome."

"I'll ask my dad to get my ticket changed."

"I can't wait. I mean I can wait on the stuff with my mom and my dad and all of that."

"That's part of it. I'm so excited. It will be good for us. 'Let's play ball!'" She laughs at herself and waves at me as she walks up the dirt road toward her cabin.

76.

Yesterday afternoon I was on the basketball court. This afternoon I'm assigned to the archery field. I've not been out here all summer. I'm not even sure how this stuff works. These are real bows and arrows. Last summer Will took down a javelina with this set.

There's never a big crowd at the archery field so I bring my notebook along. I'm getting everything set up and am surprised as Billy and Dill walk up. "Hey guys, want to shoot?"

Dill answers. Dill always answers. "We were going to get something to drink from the canteen and then go swimming. We'll come back later."

"Cool. Get me something too. You owe me Charles Harris from Yuma."

"Okay. I guess I owe you." He looks at Billy, "Let's go."

Billy is lingering a little. He's looking at me.

"Hey, Dill. I need to follow up with Billy on something for the report. I'll buy this time at the canteen if you go down there for us."

"Deal!" He nods and heads off down the dirt road.

Billy tries to smile as he comes over and sits at the empty table.

"How's your hand, dude?"

"It's good. It itches all the time and this bandage is so annoying." He starts to scratch it.

"Don't scratch it, Billy. Are you nuts?"

"Um…" He looks around. "You know…"

"What's up, Billy?"

"Nothing, really. I just wanted to say thanks for taking me to the hospital and for talking with my dad and everything. I still think he's going to kill me." He looks down.

"Tell me about life in Buckeye, Billy."

"Have you ever been to Buckeye?"

"I've been through it. It's about Buckeye where my radio goes out every time I drive through the desert. I hate that place." I laugh hoping he'll laugh with me.

He tries to laugh but can't. He can't even smile, "Life in Buckeye sucks."

"Why is that?"

"My dad and mom and all."

I look at him and he looks at me. I see a trust in his eyes that I wonder if I've ever had. "Tell me about your dad. What's the deal there?"

He hangs his head again. He mumbles, "He's mad a lot."

I reach out and grab his shoulder, "I'm sorry, Billy."

"He didn't use to be mad all the time. That thing you said in the truck the other day…the thing about parents loving in weird ways or something?"

"Ya, I think that might be right."

He quickly shoots back, "Is being hit for no reason one of those weird ways?"

He's looking intently at me. He's really asking me this. How does he not know?

"No, Billy. Being hit is never an expression of love. Never. No matter what someone says when they do it."

He hangs his head again and picks up a few rocks. He throws one toward the archery target. "Thought so."

"Great throw…Hey, it's never okay."

He throws another rock, and then another.

"It's never okay. Ever."

He throws another rock, this time harder than the one before. I lean over and find a couple of larger rocks as he throws a fourth, and fifth. His last throw was harder than the previous two combined. Tears start forming in his eyes. He quickly wipes them away and then throws another rock.

I don't say a word. He stands up and is scrambling around. He's breathing heavy. His body is all tensed up. I reach out and hand him one of my rocks. He snatches it from me and throws it as hard he can. He's seething. He looks like he's about to explode. I hand him another rock. He looks at it and throws it violently, letting out a scream that echoes through the canyon. He falls back on the bench, crossing his arms. I reach out toward him and he slides away. Other campers and staff heard his screaming and are all standing around gawking.

I start to whisper, "Whatever is going on with your dad, it's not your fault. Nothing you've done or not done makes this okay."

He looks over at me with a look of such pain, "How can you say that, you don't even know him?"

"I don't know him. I do know his anger is not because of your grades or your room or your attitude or how well your play trumpet."

He shakes his head and then looks back at me, "How do you know that?"

"I don't really know. But I do know something about anger. I bet his anger is about something deep in him or maybe something that happened to him. It's not about you." He slowly tilts his head; I can almost see his brain working to process all of this. I decide to keep going, "I bet your dad loves you. It sounds like your dad is struggling to love himself. A lot of people have that struggle."

He shakes his head quickly and huffs as tears well up. He knows people are watching but he almost yells as he responds, "He's so mean sometimes. I don't know why. I do everything right. He's just so mean. I hate him!"

I don't take my eyes off of him. He catches his breath and looks at me, and then looks around seeing people stopping and staring.

"Look at me," I say. He looks at me and then looks around again. "Don't worry about them. It's okay. You're okay."

"They all probably think I'm a freak."

Our eyes finally connect. "Nah, can I tell you what I think? I think you are heroic. Takes someone of incredible courage and strength to say what you just said." He shakes his head and hides his face with his hands.

After a few moments, he wipes his eyes, takes a quick look around, and then looks back at me. It's the signal to keep talking. I nod, "Does your mom know about all of this?"

"No. They're divorced. I only see her sometimes. My dad won't let me see her much."

"I'm so sorry. My parents are divorced too. It sucks, doesn't it?"

"They are?"

"Yep. Billy, can I ask you a weird question? Do you trust your mom?"

For the first time, he smiles a huge smile and then it quickly fades, "I do, my dad doesn't, but I do."

I nod. I keep nodding. "She needs to know."

"I want to tell her. I've wanted to tell her for so long. My dad keeps telling me that if I tell her, or anyone, that he'll kill me, and her"

"She needs to know. Now."

"You mean like right now?"

"I think so. Secrets suck, Billy. She needs to know right now."

His whole posture changes almost instantly. He looks so relieved. Like the weight of his world, no, the weight of his dad's world is lifted.

77.

Billy and I have been inseparable since the other day. We walk down to the field for the Moonlight Hike. Tonight is the last Hike of the summer. Every guy in my cabin has a date. Dill asked Laney to be his date, which she politely declined and then set him and Billy up with two sisters from El Mirage, not too far from Buckeye, not that she knew.

My guys are nervously waiting for the girls to come down. Truth is I'm as stoked as these guys as I wait for Laney.

She eventually comes down with a bunch of girls. Laney is wearing a summer dress, sandals, and her hair pulled back. Her Wayfarers sit atop, holding everything in place. She does a slight curtsey.

"You look great tonight," I say.

"Why thank you. I wanted to wear something nice for our last Moonlight Hike."

"You look amazing, just as amazing as the first Moonlight Hike when you were wearing your *Born in the USA* tour T-shirt."

"I don't know about that. Wait, you remember that?" She stares me down until I let out a laugh after being caught.

The kids are all getting connected as Pastor Wes and Mrs. Johnson make their way toward us. I figure the Johnsons are going to walk by as I haven't really spoken to them since the other day. I'm taken aback when Pastor Wes says, "You two ready for the Hike?"

Laney and I look at each other and nod, "Yes. We're pretty excited. Last Hike of the year and all."

"Great. We've been looking forward to leading this one with you."

I make a quick glance at Laney. She's smiling and nodding. "Oh, right. We are too," I say. A couple of my guys come up and pull me aside. I point to the Johnsons and say, "Excuse me a second."

"What's up guys? Everything cool?"

"Actually, not cool, John. The girls we were supposed to go with don't want to go with us anymore."

"Oh, that's not good, or maybe it is good. Listen, Pastor Wes and Mrs. Johnson were looking for some guys to help lead the Hike. You guys know the desert better than anyone. How about you guys join them up here?"

They nod excitedly, "That'd be totally awesome!"

They walk up to the Johnsons, "John says we are leading this with you. We can take it from here."

Pastor Wes looks at them and then back at me. Laney looks my way too. She stretches out her hand. A couple of other kids come up and soon there are kids everywhere. They're all excited. Pastor Wes lets out a loud call, "Let the last Moonlight Hike of the summer begin!" Cheers erupt all around.

As we walk, Laney and I invariably get separated. Each time we make it back to each other and grab hands. Pastor Wes and Mrs. Johnson try a few times to ask us questions, semi-serious questions, and every time we are pulled away, or get interrupted in mid conversation. I look for any chance not to be in this conversation. After a few attempts Mrs. Johnson slips her arm through Laney's arm signaling that she wants to talk without interruption. I slow down and get in step with the kids behind us as Pastor Wes walks with my two guys and a mob of boys up front. I watch Laney and Mrs. Johnson. Laney's totally free. She's as engaged with Mrs. Johnson as she was Billy. It's so beautiful to watch.

The Hike ends down near the creek. The moonlight is glistening on the water.

At the end of the night, as we are trying to pull our campers away from each other, I finally reconnect with Laney on the bridge, "You good?"

She smiles, "Yes, I'm really good. I missed you tonight though."

"We were going pretty good there for a minute."

"Yes, we were…you're a good guy, John."

"Ya, how so?"

"Lots of things, lots of ways."

"I want to be good. I really do. One day I will be good."

"You are good. I think we are good together."

I lean back on the rail. Laney tilts her head at me and smiles. A couple of kids come running towards us causing Laney to back up so they can run across the bridge. We watch them go by and then look each other laughing a little.

Laney rests both hands on the rail and looks up at the stars, "This is good."

78.

After loading his stuff on the bus Dill says, "I promise I'm going to go to the library and check out *To Kill a Mockingbird* as soon as I get home."

"You talk too much to read, Dill." I hug him tight, "You're a great kid, Charles Harris from Yuma. You know that? You're the best."

"Thanks, John from Camp in the Canyon," he says while getting on the bus. "That makes you second best."

Billy comes up with some new friends. His face is full and free. I grab his arm and look at his bandage, turning his hand over and back, "Not bad. I've gotten pretty good at this."

He leans to hug me. While he does I pull his rolled-up magazine out of my back pocket. I whisper in his ear and tap him on the back. "This stays in your bag, and then gets put back before your dad knows what happened."

He hugs me even bigger. I slip the magazine into his black plastic bag and tie it in a knot. We walk over and I throw the bag in the luggage compartment under the bus.

He looks at me like he's trying to say something. I speak first, "You're set then, yes? It's all worked out."

He nods his head with me, "I know. You told me the plan like five times. My mom told me too."

"Okay. Get out of here. Go be your heroic self in Buckeye."

He waves and walks toward the bus. Sadness and joy are both present here as the buses pull away. I can't decide which one I want to feel most.

Mark looks at me curiously, "Please tell me you didn't put that *Playboy* in Billy's bag."

"Then don't ask."

Pete shakes his head, "Dude, seriously? Was that the best thing you could do for him?"

"I have no idea what the best thing is for that kid. It's one less thing for him to worry about…and, there's no way I'm keeping it."

Pete lightens up, "You got that right. It's the Madonna one anyway, right?"

I smack him, "Yep. Cause you know I would have kept it if it was my girl from Bananarama."

They both push me and smack me, "It's a '*Cruel Summer*!'" they yell.

"I'm kidding. I'm kidding."

Laney is standing with a few other folks. She sees us goofing off and they all come over. "What are you guys getting into?"

I put my arm around her and look at Pete and Mark. They shake their heads and commiserate. "He's not getting into anything. He's got everything he needs," Pete says.

79.

"The schedule says we have an afternoon debrief, a big gathering at the chapel, and then a Moonlight Swim. There's a note at the bottom that says, 'Please be prepared to fully engage each portion of the next 24 hours.'" Mark looks back at Pete who's been reading over his shoulder.

Pete points at the paper, "Pastor Wes knows a bunch of people are already checked out. My brother's been checked out for about two weeks."

Not waiting for us to finish eating, Andee grabs the microphone, "Let me interrupt as I want to make sure you all know where your debrief locations are. Meetings will begin immediately after lunch. Boys counselors will meet with the Johnsons at the picnic tables."

Andee keeps talking while the guys and I exchange looks. I whisper to them, "Do we have to be so freaking dramatic all the time?"

"Seriously," Mark says.

Pete tries to calm us, "Come on guys. Let's finish well."

"You're dismissed. Enjoy your meetings," Andee says.

We stop and shoot baskets. I'm stalling us as long as possible.

80.

We are telling Eddie Murphy jokes as we walk up the dirt road to the meeting. At one point Pete's laughing so hard he has to stop walking. He bends over, putting his hands on his knees, trying to catch his breath in between gasps. We haven't laughed like this since Will left. It feels so good.

The Johnsons are already at the table when we finally walk up. The irony of all this is now laughable. Pete and Mark slowly begin to dial in. "Let's get this over with," I whisper.

Pastor Wes looks at Mrs. Johnson, then back at us as we sit down. "Guys, thanks for meeting us. And thanks for meeting us here. We know this is one of your favorite spots so we chose this spot to honor that, to honor you."

Pete nods and says, "Oh, that's awesome."

Mark says, "Thanks." He looks at me. I look back at him but don't say a word.

Pete is paying no attention to Mark and me. He says, "To be honest, it's not that this table is special, it's the guys that sit around it, or used to sit around it."

I look in amazement at Pete. That sounded like a shot at the Johnsons. I look at Mark to catch his eye, but he avoids me.

"That's right," Mrs. Johnson says. "You are exactly right. We can accept that sentiment, Pete. That's in part why we wanted to talk with you. As we've sorted through the accusations and the actual policy violations, and in talking with Mike at Wagon Wheel, and mostly through our own conversation, we've come to understand that we've treated you unfairly."

Pastor Wes joins her, "And one of the things we've discerned is that William chose to become the scapegoat. He took blame that wasn't his to take to protect those girls. I wish he wouldn't have done that, but he did."

I can hardly sit still, "Pastor Wes, I'm glad you said that, but Will didn't have a choice. For the last couple of summers he's been blamed for things he didn't do, and he knew there was no way the truth would see the light of day. I'm angry he made the decision he did and took the blame for whatever you think happened, but I'm sure he did it because he knew you wouldn't believe the truth."

Mark taps my leg to signal me to calm down. I know he's right. I know he is. But this has been so wrong for so long.

"I understand your frustration, John. The truth is you are probably right. We didn't believe him."

Mrs. Johnson looks at all three of us and then back at me. "No, we didn't believe him…I didn't believe him. I was wrong."

Pastor Wes slides his hand onto Mrs. Johnsons hand. "*We* were wrong. We have called William and told him we were wrong."

Pete smiles and nods, "That's so rad. I'm glad you did that. That was the right thing to do."

The table goes silent. It doesn't become an "awkward silence"; it's way past awkward. Pastor Wes looks at Mrs. Johnson. She looks over at Pete and leans forward, "Sweet Pete, one of the things I've noticed about you since the first day of summer was your joy. It breaks my heart to know that I've dampened your joy by my actions. I was wrong. I'm sorry."

Pete nods again. He smiles his big smile, "It's okay, Mrs. Johnson. I knew once you found the truth it would all change. Thanks. You don't have to be sorry."

She looks at Mark. She reaches her hands across the table and rests them on his hands. I start to squirm. This is so textbook. This is my mom at her absolute Sunday worst. "Mark, I am sorry. You are one of the smartest and most caring boys I know. You love your friends so well. I am sorry for all the hurt and frustration I caused."

Mark is not as sweet as Pete. "Thanks so much. The wound still stings, I know it will heal. Thanks for saying something."

I can feel every fiber of me bulking up. This is total b.s. Here it comes.

Pastor Wes mercifully intervenes, if only for a moment. "Boys, I too was wrong. I was wrong about you. I am so sorry."

Then the inevitable, Mrs. Johnson looks at me, "John, I said some very hurtful things to you the other day. I spoke out of my own hurt. Regardless, I was wrong and I'm so very sorry."

I nod and flash a fake smile to get this over with. I'm so sick of this. It's so freaking old.

Mark speaks for us, "Thank you both very much. We know it's been hard for you guys. We also know we've done some things that weren't totally cool. I just wish it didn't have to end up like this." He wants to say more. He can see the Johnsons are sorry. He looks at me and Will and then back at them. "We accept your apologies." Mark nods and the three of us begin to stand.

Pastor Wes smiles and motions for us to sit. "Thank you, each one of you, sincerely. We'd like to do one other thing. See, we know that what was done to William, and to you guys, especially you John, was not only wrong, it was sin. So, we want to ask you for forgiveness."

Mrs. Johnson looks at me. I look down. "John, I'm sorry for the hurt I've caused. I know I've sinned against you. So, I want to ask you for forgiveness."

I have no response. I don't know what to do with that. Mark looks at me, and I look at him and then back at Pastor Wes. I can't look at Mrs. Johnson.

The silence doesn't last. Pastor Wes pushes into it, "We love you guys. We want you to know it. And, we want you to allow us to express our love for you. In an act of repentance, we want to wash your feet."

Mark says it before I can even think it, "That's not necessary. We know you're sincere."

Pastor Wes keeps going, "It's not necessary, Mark. You're right. We want to do this. We want to express our love to you this way, and we want you to receive it, as you are able."

Pastor Wes reaches under the bench and pulls out a bucket of water. Mrs.

Johnson grabs a few towels that have been resting on her lap. They get up and come around our side of the table. Pastor Wes kicks off his flip flops. Mark and Pete swing toward them. I don't want to move, but something moves me. I turn half way just to keep watch.

Pastor Wes kneels in front of Pete and starts untying his shoes. Pete begins to break down.

Mrs. Johnson whispers something in Mark's ear. All I can hear is Pete crying.

Pastor Wes starts speaking to Pete while dipping his feet in the bucket, "God, bless these feet. Bless where they walk."

Mrs. Johnson says something similar, "This ground is holy ground, because Mark, you are holy." Mark starts crying.

I watch for as long as I can and then look away. I close my eyes, hoping to hold back whatever in me is trying to surface.

I finally open my eyes to see Pete embrace Pastor Wes. They're both crying. Soon Mrs. Johnson follows. "I love you, Mark. You are the real deal." Mark embraces her. I know they are not going to skip me, and I know I can't run.

Both Pastor Wes and Mrs. Johnson kneel down in front of me. Mark and Pete are still crying and now are hugging each other.

Mrs. Johnson speaks first as Pastor Wes slides off my flip flops, "Will you forgive me? I have sinned against you, and I have sinned against your parents. And I know I've also sinned against Davis too."

I'm crushed. The thought of Davis and all the hurt he faces, all the weight he carries, the thought of someone asking for forgiveness for hurting him kills me. I begin to come undone.

Pastor Wes leans in and speaks softly, "We know that we have sinned against you, John. We ask you for forgiveness." As he's talking Mark slips his arm around me and holds me tight. Pete crawls on the table and is now directly behind me. He's holding Mark with one hand and me with the other and I can hear him praying.

Mrs. Johnson is crying and Pastor Wes chokes up. "John, I want you to look at me."

I raise my head up to see his eyes full of tears, and drop my head, "I don't deserve this."

"Look at me John."

"I can't. If you knew what I've done…no."

"John, please look at me." Mrs. Johnson is wiping my feet, whispering a prayer. Pastor Wes speaks as if something is speaking to him as he speaks to me. "John, I want to ask forgiveness on behalf of the Church. It's not just my wife and I who have sinned against you and your family. The Church has sinned against you and your family. Please, John, forgive me, and Sheri, and Dr. Ron, and the entire Church for sinning against your family."

I wipe tears as fast as I can, trying not to look at him.

"John, I believe there is an even deeper pain in you, a pain deeper than the horrific pain you feel because of your parent's story. Something in your story."

I look at Pete and Mark and tears come rushing from the most painful place inside of me.

"For that hurt, whatever hurt that is, I want to ask you for forgiveness. Will you forgive me, forgive us?" He starts to cry. He slows only to take a breath. "I know you don't have to forgive God, but I want you to know God's heart is broken for whatever it is that happened to you. Please forgive in order to let all of this go." Tears pour out of his eyes and down his cheeks falling off his face."

I crumble into Mark's chest. I don't speak. I can't.

The Johnsons pray together for a moment. Pete now is praying louder over Mark and me. Pastor Wes begins to dry my feet and slips my flip flops back on.

Mrs. Johnson stands up and leans in to hug me, "I love you, John."

Pastor Wes pushes up the sleeves of his sweatshirt as he stands and then places both hands on my shoulders. I reach up and hold his arm. "John, you are His beloved, and with you He is well pleased." He kisses me on the top of my head and gently hugs me and then hugs the other guys, then they walk away.

I can hardly breathe. I've never felt anything so intense. I can't even describe the places both near and far from me, and the heights and depths inside of me that have been touched by all of this.

We sit in it together for a while. I don't know how long.

Pete falls onto the table and exhales and smiles.

Mark and I turn to see what he's doing. Mark says simply, "That was cool."

"Incredibly cool," Pete says, "That was amazing. I so wish Will could have been here. That would have been so rad."

They both look at me. I wipe my face, "I have no idea what just happened. I honestly don't know what to do with that. I am so freaking lost, in a good way, I guess. I don't know."

Pete sees me trying to make sense of it all and says, "Let it be what it is, whatever it is."

I stand up, "The stuff about Davis? Forgiveness on behalf of the Church? Forgiveness for…I don't even know."

81.

"Hey Davis. What's up Lil' Bro?" my voice cracking as I speak.

"What's up, Big? You headed home?"

"Ya, man. I'll be home later tomorrow night. Stopping at Ms. Audrey's for lunch."

"Oh, awesome. Tell her I said hello. Is Laney still planning on coming?"

"Yep. I'm so stoked for you to meet her."

"For sure. Me too. Then what's up?"

I see Pastor Wes and Mrs. Johnson walking hand in hand past the window of the office. Someone shouts for Pastor Wes, he smiles and waves.

"Man, Davis…I don't know…I just…I just wanted to tell you I love you and everything."

"I know that Big. I always know that."

I choke back tears. "I just wanted to be sure I told you, today."

"Okay, cool. Well, thanks. Love you too…you okay?"

I try and laugh. "Man, it's good. I just had this overwhelming thing in me, like I needed to talk with you today. That's all. I know it's weird. It's cool. I just wanted you to know."

"Thanks for calling. I'll see you tomorrow night…should I call Dawn too and let her know you're coming home? Do like a big welcome home party?" He laughs.

"Oh, come on now!"

"Gotcha Big!"

82.

The sounds of The Beach Boys and flying beach balls welcome us as we enter the Chapel. It feels more like the first day of camp than the last night of the summer. A few kids from the kitchen are dancing and singing. I totally expected quiet music and candles. We've walked into "Beach Blanket Bingo."

Pete and Beth lead us in the loudest and fastest songs that we sing. Pete waves Mark up to lead us in the "Jesus Chant." Laney is having a total blast. She's yelling as loud as she can. After watching her for a few moments I know exactly what she was like as a little girl. Watching her frees me to fully join in. By the time the chorus ends, she and I are shouting back and forth at each other.

Pastor Wes eventually brings us back around to reflection, "I'd like to invite you to briefly share some victory stories from the summer. You can share about a victory from one of your campers, but I'd rather you share a victory in your story."

Brian, from the kitchen, gets up, "I really learned a lot about forgiveness." He looks at the Johnsons. "Thanks for forgiving me, Pastor Wes."

We clap as Brian sits down, joining the other kids from the kitchen. They all pat him on the back.

Eileen stands up, "My love for beauty has been awakened again. Life had become so black and white for so long. Today it's glorious." We all clap as she sits down. A couple of other people share.

"One more, maybe?" Pastor Wes says. Everyone sits in the uncomfortable silence. Just as it's about to end, Marcie jumps to her feet.

"I need to say something. I know I haven't said much, especially since Will left." She forces a smile. "My story has been really hard – long before Will left. I just want to say that I've been lost for a long time and I really want to go home." She hesitates. "I'm learning that it's not only kids who go totally crazy who are lost. Some of us who stay around home and don't really go anywhere can be just as lost. I've been lost in my anger and doubt and comparison for a long, long, time. I've blamed myself, I've tormented myself, I've even hated myself. I'm so lost. I want to be found."

As abruptly as she got up, she sits down. We all clap, this time we are in a bit of awe. Laney sitting next to her, doesn't say anything to her. They wrap their arms around each other and Laney whispers in her ear. Watching them love each other… it's like the painting.

Pastor Wes sees what's opening up before him, "Thank you, Marcie. Anyone else ready to come home?" A few kids from the kitchen raise their hands. Some others nod. Danny gets up and walks down to the altar at the front. Other kids start to join him. Marcie gets up and motions for Laney to come forward with her. Beth and Vista follow them. There is no room at the altar so they kneel at some chairs in the first couple of rows. Mrs. Johnson is working her way around to different kids. Pastor Wes stands with his arms open and his head tilted toward heaven.

Pete pulls Mark and me in. We scoot our seats together and both guys pray out loud the most personal prayers for themselves and for their families. It's so deep. So honest. And then we are quiet. The room is not quiet. All around us prayers are rising, but we are quiet. We sit in our quiet. We know it's okay to sit in our silence. It feels true and right like this.

The girls come back and instead of sitting in their seats they sort of huddle up around us. The three of us guys surrounded by these four girls. I know it should probably be the other way around; maybe for now this is the way it's supposed to be.

Vista exhales, you can almost hear a smile come over her face, "God, guide Mark as he goes back to school. May your hand be on his heart and on his mind and on his soul. Amen."

Beth starts praying for Pete. While she's praying I start to wonder if Laney is going to pray for me. I wonder if I should pray for her.

Marcie prays next, "God, will you remind Will that we all love him and that we miss him. Amen."

It's quiet for a few moments. Laney rests her hands on my shoulders. She starts whispering, but not to me.

Pete prays aloud, "God, bring us all home. Bring me home. Bring all these guys with me, Will too. Bring us to your table, to your party. Help us all be okay there, with you. Amen."

We get up and start hugging each other.

I grab Marcie first, "You're the best. I'm so thankful for you. I'm glad you're coming home."

She clutches me, "Thank you for being a good friend to Will, and to me." She kisses me on the cheek and says, "I hope we can be home together."

As Laney hugs Marcie, my eyes catch the cross at the front of the room.

Laney wipes tears from her eyes. She tries to smile, "Hey, can we talk for a minute? There's something about me I haven't told you."

83.

I point to the back of the chapel and grab her hand. We walk back and then turn two seats toward each other to sit face to face. She leans toward me, resting her elbows on her knees. She looks at me and tears again begin to run down her face.

I sit tight not touching her but trying to hold all of her.

Her tears turn to cries – cries of the heart.

I slide my chair over and put my arm around her.

"I've done some terrible things," she says in between shakes and sobs.

I gently reach over and rub her back.

She sits up and falls in my arms all in one motion.

Through her cries she says, "I know I'm forgiven, but it still hurts so much."

I hold her tight and she holds me tight.

I wipe the hair out her face so I can see her face. She rubs the tears from under her eyes. "I've never told anyone about it," she says trembling.

"It's okay. You're okay."

"I don't even know where to start. It's all so much."

"What did you tell me the other night? You said, 'I'm here. I'm not going anywhere.' Hear me say it to you now, I'm here."

"John, I'm sorry if this is all too much, if I'm too much."

"You're not too much. You are enough." She doesn't say anything. She doesn't cry or smile or turn away. She looks right at me. Her eyes tell me she understands.

Someone turns on the music. The Beach Boys start to sing over us. A beach ball lands right next to us.

She leans in to speak over the music, "I heard Pastor Wes the other night. He said, 'there's no fear in love.' I've been wanting to tell you all summer, but I wasn't sure."

I wipe some tears from my eyes and look into hers. I put my hand on her shoulder, "He's right, Laney. There's no fear in love. You don't have to be afraid."

Mark and Pete and a bunch of kids start dancing. Laney turns and looks over her shoulder. Her lip is still trembling as she says, "I know it's not a mosh pit, but will you dance with me?"

84.

"You lack nothing."

Pastor Wes is taking his time, looking each person in the eyes, resting his hands on their shoulders, offering his blessing.

I'm trying to hustle us along as Laney and I are detouring at Ms. Audrey's for lunch and then meeting the rest of the group at the beach. Will's already there.

Laney gets stopped by Eileen. Marcie comes toward me, singing, *"Goodbye everybody I've got to go / Gotta leave you all behind and face the truth."* We keep singing Queen as we walk through the parking lot. Marcie too gets stopped and that leaves me as a sitting target as Andee walks toward me. She doesn't say anything at first. There's no way I'm saying anything. She leans toward me and reaches out her hand. It takes everything in me to shake her hand. For the first time, she smiles an almost genuine smile, "I hope you'll come back next summer."

I smile an almost genuine smile. "Thanks…hey, can I say thanks for letting me take Billy to the hospital the other day. You could have stopped that, and you didn't. That was super cool."

"You were the best person to be with him. I knew that. Hope you'll come back."

I turn away as Marcie walks by. She whispers, "Did she just really say what I think she did?'"

"Unbelievable…I'm only coming back if you are."

We laugh together and hug, "Have fun at the beach," she says.

She and Laney laugh and cry at the same time as they hug goodbye.

Laney hands me her backpack and wipes her face. I move slowly toward my truck and open the passenger door, giving her a moment with Andee and then Mrs. Johnson as she too waits patiently to say her goodbyes to Laney. I throw her backpack on the seat next to my shoebox of cassettes that now is also stuffed full of letters from campers, my notebook, and Jimmy's rosary beads. My copy of *The Last Battle* sits on top of all of it. I hate that I didn't finish the book with my guys. The ending is the best part.

Laney wipes the last few tears from her eyes and smiles at me as she walks around the truck and gets in. Mrs. Johnson waves at both of us. I close the door and take a last look around as I walk slowly back to my side. It's a pretty rad sight.

"We lack nothing," Laney says as we pull out on the dirt road along the creek, through the gate and into the canyon.

85.

Ms. Audrey is working in her cactus pots as we pull up. She waves excitedly as she takes off her gloves. She comes around my side of the truck and is at the door before I get out.

"Welcome home, John. I'm so glad you are here." She gives me the biggest hug.

"It's so good to see you Ms. Audrey. Thanks for making time for us today."

She slips her arm through mine as we walk slowly around the truck together.

Laney and Ms. Audrey hug without saying a word.

"I'm so glad to finally meet you, Laney."

"I'm glad to finally meet you too, Ms. Audrey. I've heard so much about you."

"You two come in, come in. Now, I know you don't have much time, but John, I've made your favorite."

She leads us straight into her tiny dining room.

"Oh, no way! This is my favorite meal. This is awesome. Thanks so much."

We sit down to the most appetizing meal of the summer. The table setting itself would be enough, with candles, china, and folded napkins. And the food…the food is incredible. We have roast beef, Yorkshire pudding, warm crescent rolls, trifle, and glass bottled Cokes.

As we talk I learn some things about Laney I didn't know. Her mom picked cotton alongside sharecroppers in the Mississippi Delta, and not surprisingly, she's never had Yorkshire pudding. "This is delicious. I'd love to learn how to make this," she says.

"It's an art, Laney. I learned it from John's mom. I'll teach you the secret. What about you, John? What did you learn about yourself this summer?"

"What did I learn about myself…that's big. A lot, actually. One thing I learned is I want to be good. I want the bad to be gone so I can be good. And I don't want to be afraid. I don't want to be afraid anymore…I guess that's two things."

Laney turns my way. She's learning some things about me too.

Ms. Audrey smiles at me and plainly says, "You are good, John. You are good."

Laney pats me on my leg, "I think so too."

The conversation thankfully goes back to Laney, "What are you excited to see in California, Laney."

"I can't wait to see the beach, and Disneyland of course, but I think I'm most looking forward to meeting Davis."

Ms. Audrey looks at me and back at Laney "He's the best, Laney."

"Yep. He's going to meet us at the pizza place up the street from the Seal

Beach Pier, Ms. Audrey. You remember it?"

"I do. You, me and Davis ate a whole pizza there last time I visited! Laney, you will love it."

Ms. Audrey leans in. Her elbow now resting on the table, her arm straight up and she has one finger up. "John." She nods. "John, what did you mean a moment ago, when you talked about wanting to be good? Go back to that."

"Sure. I was saying, or I think I was saying I want to be good, like the way God would want me to be good. I've never figured out how to do that. I still don't know. I want to learn to be good."

Laney is taking this all in. Ms. Audrey has my full attention.

"You are learning how to be good…" she says. She puts her napkin in her lap and looks at me with the most beautiful look I've ever seen. I'm awestruck. And then she says it. Sitting right here on a Wednesday afternoon, eating Yorkshire pudding. "John. You are good. You don't have to learn how to be good. You are good! His love makes you good, in the middle of all the bad. John, God doesn't have any expectations of you. Do you know that? He just loves you. Just as you are, right where you are. He just wants to be with you."

Then she gets up and starts clearing the table. Laney follows. There are tears in Laney's eyes too. Then a smile, as if she's totally got it figured out, which I'm sure she does. She grabs our plates and goes to help in the kitchen.

"I'm good even though there's bad… God doesn't have any expectations of me? He just loves me? He just wants to be with me?"

86.

"She's even more angelic than you described, John. What a beautiful soul."

"There's no one on the planet like her."

The radio begins to disconnect from the station. I point to the shoebox full of cassettes, "You up for being our desert DJ?"

"Of course, I always wanted to be a DJ." She flips through a few tapes. "No Bruce Springsteen I see. I know what I'm giving you for Christmas."

"That would be a great gift."

She grabs Stevie Ray Vaughan, "Here we go." She opens the cassette and pops it in the player, "This is Laney Chapman bringing the delta blues to the scorching Arizona desert."

We sing "Pride and Joy" the only song we both know.

Eventually, she pulls out *Crime and Punishment*. "I've got to finish this, write a paper, and have it postmarked by Labor Day."

"That book is such a beast." I point to *The Last Battle* on the top of the box, "That one is a whole lot shorter. Maybe you could write about that instead."

"I wish." She picks up *The Last Battle* and smiles when she sees the rosary beads. She pulls them out of the box too. "These remind you of Lonny?"

"I love that kid, and his homies. Billy and Dill too"

"I know you do. I love that about you…whoops, this picture slid out of your book."

"Oh, it's my bookmark."

She picks up the photograph from the floorboard and looks at it, "John, look at how young you are."

"That was a long time ago."

"How old are you here? And this must be Davis. How old is he?"

"I was like, seven or eight. Davis would be five or six."

"You use this picture as a bookmark? Tell me about that."

Tears want to well up in my eyes. I try to laugh them away. She sees me and rests her hand on my leg.

I put my hand on hers, interlocking our fingers, "That was us. At our best." She looks at the photograph and then back at me. She doesn't just look at me, she sees me. She sees me.

"Where are you, John?"

"We were like four chapters from the end," I say quickly. "I was so close to finishing. I couldn't keep my eyes open on the last night of camp. All my guys had fallen asleep anyway."

"That's not what I mean."

"I know it's not." I look at her. "I'm here."

"I'm here too."

A few miles later she opens *The Last Battle*, "I remember this having the best ending, but I can't remember it."

"Oh, no way. Read the last few paragraphs of the book. It's killer."

She turns the pages slowly, still holding the photograph between her fingers. She looks at me with her one eye brow raised, "You mean this part that looks like it's been underlined like five different times?"

"It's the best."

She starts to read, *"But the things that began to happen after that were so great and beautiful that I cannot write them. And for us this is the end of all the stories, and we can most truly say that they all lived happily ever after. But for them it was only the beginning of the real story. All their life in this world and all their adventures in Narnia had only been the cover and the title page; now at last they were beginning Chapter One of the Great Story, which no one on earth has read; which goes on forever; in which every chapter is better than the one before."*

She closes the book, still holding the photograph, and looks over. "That's pretty incredible."

I place my hand on hers, look out the widow, and smile.

We ride passing cactus and sagebrush and deserted gas stations. It all looks the same and yet so very different. The past tries to creep in a few times and even that which is ahead wants to haunt and threaten but it won't have its way. I'm home in my own skin in a place that never felt like home.

"Hey, John, what about your story? How's that coming along"? she says as we ride past the sign, "Quartzite 80 miles."

www.ingramcontent.com/pod-product-compliance
Lightning Source LLC
Chambersburg PA
CBHW010640100726
47900CB00011B/2909